THE BRAZILIAN TYCOON'S MISTRESS

BY

FIONA HOOD-STEWART

MILLS & BOON®

*First published in Great Britain 2004
Large Print edition 2005
Harlequin Mills & Boon Limited,
Eton House, 18-24 Paradise Road,
Richmond, Surrey TW9 1SR*

© Fiona Hood-Stewart 2004

ISBN 0 263 18541 9

*Set in Times Roman 16½ on 17½ pt.
16-0405-52864*

*Printed and bound in Great Britain
by Antony Rowe Ltd, Chippenham, Wiltshire*

CHAPTER ONE

IT WAS a grey Tuesday afternoon in October when Araminta Dampierre, abstractedly parking her old Land Rover in front of the village shop, felt a jolt and heard a thud. With a sinking heart she twisted her head. Close behind her stood a four-wheel drive that she'd just hit.

With a sigh Araminta climbed out of her vehicle and took stock of the gleaming silver Range Rover's squished bumper. Her own Land Rover was not in a great state anyway, but this Range Rover had been in pristine condition—obviously the latest model, and brand-new. Wishing she'd paid more attention to her surroundings, Araminta looked up and down the empty village street, searching for a possible owner. But there was no one to be seen.

Taking a last reluctant look at the damage she'd done, Araminta decided to proceed with her shopping and wait and see if the owner of the Range Rover appeared. Maybe the proprietor of the glistening vehicle that she was fast beginning to loathe would have returned by then, no doubt filled with much righteous indignation.

As she turned to head towards the grocer's she visualised a dreadfully chic corporate wife—with whom Sussex seemed to be teeming lately—complaining furiously about her careless behaviour.

At the grocer's Araminta handed her shopping list to dear old Mr Thompson and waited patiently while he shuffled about the shelves in search of several items.

'And how is Her Ladyship?' the white-haired bespectacled grocer asked solicitously.

'My mother is fine, thank you,' Araminta responded, smiling. 'She's recovered after that bout of bronchitis.'

'Well, thank goodness for that. A bad spell it was. My wife had it too.'

'I'm so sorry,' Araminta murmured, glancing out of the window back towards the cars, hoping she wouldn't have to hear all the details of Mrs Thompson's illness.

'Will that be all?' Mr Thompson smiled benignly from across the counter at Araminta, whom he had known since she was a small child, when she'd come in after going to the Pony Club to buy sweets.

'Thanks, I think that's everything. Just pop it onto the account as usual, will you? And do send my best to Mrs Thompson. I hope she makes a quick recovery.'

'Thank you, miss, I will.'

Araminta stepped back onto the pavement, brown paper bag held under her arm, thinking how quaint it was that the villagers still called her 'miss', even though she was twenty-eight and had been married and widowed.

She made her way back to the car, deposited her bag of shopping on the passenger seat, and wondered what to do, since there was still no sign of the driver of the Range Rover. For all she knew, she or he might not appear for ages. She could hardly stand around waiting all afternoon.

With a reluctant sigh Araminta took out a pad and pen from her well-worn Hermès bag and scribbled what she hoped was a legible note, which she slipped behind the windscreen wiper of the Range Rover. There was little else she could do. The driver could get in touch with her and they could exchange information about their respective insurance companies over the phone.

*   *   *

'I'm back!' Araminta called round the drawing room door of Taverstock Hall to where her mother sat reading by the fire.

'Ah. Good. I've just told Olive to bring in tea.'

'Okay, I'll be down in a minute. Just popping the groceries into the pantry. Mr Thompson sends his best, by the way.'

'Ah. Thank you.' Lady Drusilla inclined her head graciously. 'I really must do something about the Christmas bazaar. Perhaps you could help, Araminta? Instead of scribbling away at those wretched children's books of yours. It's time you pulled yourself together and did something useful. After all, when your father died I didn't spend *my* time drifting. I took charge.'

'Mother, please don't let's get into this again.'

'Oh, very well.' Lady Drusilla cast her eyes heavenwards and Araminta made good her escape.

She really must set about finding a place of her own again, she reflected as she descended the back stairs and popped the bag on the pantry table. It was her own fault that she was subjecting herself to her mother's endless comments. But she just hadn't been able to face—or afford—staying in the house she'd lived in with Peter. It had taken all her will-power to get the strength together to clear it up and put it on the market, and be able to unload the mortgage. Still, it was time, she knew, to move on.

The first thing Victor Santander saw as he walked towards his new Range Rover was the gaping dent in the right bumper. With a muffled exclamation he moved forward and inspected it closely. Some idiot had backed into him and hadn't had the courtesy to wait and own up. He crouched, studied the dent, and realised that the whole bumper would need replacing.

He rose with an annoyed sigh, and then noticed the note flapping behind the windscreen wiper. At least the perpetrator had had the decency to leave a phone number, he noted, slightly mollified by the apology. It was signed 'A. Dampierre'. No Mr or Miss or Mrs. Just the initial.

Oh, well, he supposed he'd better give A. Dampierre a call once he got home to Chippenham Manor, which he'd moved into the day before. An accident on his first day in this quaint English village didn't bode too well for the future.

Usually when he drove down the country lane Victor enjoyed the sight of the rolling hills, the trimmed hedges and the horses grazing in the fields. But not after the car incident. And the weather was foul. Yet it suited his mood, he reflected sombrely. So much better than the blaring sun of his homeland, which, for now, he could do without.

At least here he could lick his wounds in peace and quiet, without having to undergo the social scandal that would inevitably be his lot in Rio de Janeiro once Isabella's latest affair became known. At least here he would be left alone.

Back at the Manor he entered the hall and was greeted by loud barks. He smiled as Lolo, his golden retriever, came frolicking across the oriental carpet, thrilled at her master's return.

'*Calma, linda,*' he said stroking the dog's head and heading towards the study. 'You'll get used to living in a large English country house. Surely you'll like it better than the penthouse in Rio?' he murmured, suddenly remembering his vast, white-marbled modern apartment in Ipanema, glad he was far away from it and all the horror of his soon-to-be ex-wife's unwelcome surprises. This was about as far removed as he could get from Isabella, both physically and mentally, he reflected, entering the study.

In fact, nowhere could be far enough, he added to himself, pulling out the crumpled note from his pocket and glancing briefly at it. He realised he'd better give A. Dampierre a call right away and sort the mess out.

Stifling his irritation, he sat down at the large partner's desk, covered with files and photographs of racehorses, and dialled the number, noting that A. Dampierre must be a local, since he had the same area code. Probably some careless local farmer.

The number rang several times.

'Hello, Taverstock Hall,' an aristocratic female voice answered.

'Good afternoon. Could I speak to…' He hesitated. 'A. Dampierre?'

'A Dampierre?' the haughty female voice replied.

'Yes, I was referring to the initial A,' he replied, in arctic tones.

'The initial— Oh, I suppose you must be referring to— Hold on a moment, would you?' He heard a muffled sound in the distance.

'Hello?' Another, much softer female voice came on the line, and for some reason he could not define Victor was surprised to find that 'A' was a woman. He really had imagined a burly red-faced farmer. This voice certainly did not match that image! But neither did it diminish his annoyance.

'Excuse me, madam, I had a note left on my windscreen by A. Dampierre. Is that you?'

'Oh, yes. The bumper. Look, I'm really sorry about what happened. I backed into your car by mistake, you see.'

'In no uncertain terms,' he muttered dryly.

'I wasn't paying proper attention, I'm afraid,' the female voice murmured apologetically.

'That,' he remarked wryly, 'has become abundantly clear.'

'Well, I'm sure my insurance company will deal with it,' replied the woman's voice, now slightly less apologetic.

'Of course,' he said dismissively.

'I'm sorry to have put you to all this inconvenience,' she continued, her tone definitely chillier. 'If there is anything I can do to be of assistance...' Her voice trailed off.

'I don't think there is.'

'Perhaps I could give my insurance company a call immediately and explain?'

Victor's eyes narrowed and he hesitated a moment. Then curiosity got the better of him and his lips curved. 'Perhaps it would be preferable if we met, and then I could give you my insurance information.'

A hesitation followed. 'All right. When would suit you?'

Victor thought. He really had nothing to do now that he'd moved in and his horses were safely ensconced at the training farm a few miles down the road. And for some inexplicable reason this voice intrigued him.

'How about tomorrow morning?'

'Fine. Would ten o'clock do?'

'Okay. But not in front of the grocer's, if you don't mind,' he added with a touch of humour.

A delicious tinkling laugh echoed down the line. 'No, I think better not. Where are you exactly?'

'I'm at Chippenham Manor.'

'At Chip— Oh! I see. So in fact you're our new neighbour.'

'Neighbour?'

'Yes. I live at Taverstock Hall. Our property shares a boundary with yours.'

'Ah. I see. Then it is high time we introduced ourselves,' Victor said, wondering if someone with such a charming voice might turn out to be sixty-five, fat and have a double chin. Serve him right if she did. 'Victor Santander, at your service.'

'Uh, Araminta Dampierre.'

'A pleasure. Shall I come over to the Hall at ten o'clock, then?'

'Um…if you don't mind I'll pop over to the Manor. I have to go out around that time anyway,' she said hurriedly.

'As you wish. I shall expect you at ten.'

'And again, I'm very sorry about your bumper.'

'Don't be. The damage is done, so there is little use in being sorry. Until tomorrow.'

He hung up and glanced at the picture of Copacabana Baby, his favourite filly, wondering why the woman had so definitely not wanted him to go over to Taverstock Hall.

Maybe she had a difficult husband who would give her hell because she'd had an accident.

Then he let out a sigh and got up to pour himself a whisky before settling down to study the future of two of his horses which he kept at his stud near Deauville.

'Who on earth was that odd-sounding man on the phone?' Lady Drusilla demanded, gazing in a speculative manner at the platter of fresh scones baked earlier in the day by Olive.

'Oh, he's our new neighbour at the Manor. He sounds rather autocratic.'

'Hmm. Very odd indeed. Foreign, if you ask me. A. Dampierre, indeed. What a strange way to ask for you.'

'It wasn't his fault. I left a note for him on his windscreen and I must have signed it A. Dampierre.'

'A note on a strange man's windscreen?' Lady Drusilla raised horrified brows. 'Really, Araminta, whatever were you thinking of?'

'I bumped into his car by mistake,' Araminta explained patiently, sweeping her long ash-blonde mane off her shoulders and leaning over to pour the tea.

'How extremely careless of you.'

'I'm very well aware of that,' she said tightly. 'Actually, he was very nice about it.'

'So he should be. It's not every day he'll have the privilege of being bumped into by a Taverstock, as it were.'

'Mother, why must you be so pompous?' Araminta exclaimed, her dark blue eyes flashing at her mother's ridiculous statement.

'I shall have to find out from Marion Nethersmith who he is, exactly, and what is going on at the Manor,' Lady Drusilla continued as though her daughter hadn't spoken. 'It's been quite a mystery. Nobody knew who was moving in. I think it's too bad that one doesn't know anything about one's neighbours any more. They might be anybody.'

'Well, I'll know soon enough,' Araminta said shortly. 'I'm due over there with my car insurance information to settle this matter tomorrow at ten.'

'Really, Araminta, I find it hard to believe that you, a married woman—a widow, rather—who should know better, are belittling yourself in this manner. Why didn't you tell him to come here?'

'Because—' Araminta had been about to say, *I wouldn't subject anyone, let alone a stranger, to your intolerable manners.* But instead she shut up and shrugged. 'I have to go into the village anyway.

'Oh, very well. Pass me a scone, would you, dear? I know I shouldn't, but I don't suppose one can do much harm.'

CHAPTER TWO

AT TEN o'clock precisely, Araminta, clad in a pair of worn jeans, an Arran sweater, a Barbour rain jacket and Wellington boots, pulled up on the gravel in front of Chippenham Manor, noting that the gardens which for ages had run wild were carefully weeded, the hedges neatly trimmed and the gravel raked. Whoever Mr Santander was, he obviously liked things in good order.

For some reason this left her feeling less daunted. It was reassuring to see the Manor—abandoned and forlorn for so long after Sir Edward's death, ignored by the distant cousin who'd inherited and whose only interest in the property had been to sell it—being properly looked after by the new owner.

Jumping out of the old Land Rover, Araminta winced at the sight of the crushed bumper on the smart new Range Rover parked next to a shining Bentley. With a sigh she walked up the steps and rang the bell. It was answered several moments later by a tanned man in uniform.

'Mr Santander is expecting me,' she said, surprised at the man's elegance. Chippenham Manor was a large, comfortable English home, but one didn't quite expect uniformed staff answering the door.

'Mrs Dampierre?' the man asked respectfully.

'Yes, that's right.'

'Please follow me.' The manservant stood back, holding the door wide, and bowed her in.

Araminta stood and stared for a full minute, barely recognizing her surroundings. The hall had been completely redecorated. She'd heard there was work going on at the Manor, but nobody knew much about it as all the firms employed had come from London.

She looked about her, impressed, enchanted by the attractive wall covering, the contemporary sconces, the bright flashes of unusual art. A particularly attractive flower arrangement stood on a drum table in the centre of the dazzling white marble floor which in Sir Edward's day had looked worn and somewhat

grubby, and which his housekeeper had com-
plained bitterly about.

'This way, madam,' the servant said, leading
her down the passage towards the drawing
room.

When she reached the threshold Araminta
gasped in sheer amazement. Gone were the
drab, musty Adam green brocade wall cover-
ings, the drooping fringed curtains and the
gloomy portraits of Sir Edward's none too prepossessing ancestors. Instead she was greeted
by soft eggshell paint, white curtains that
broke on the gleaming parquet floor, wide contemporary sofas piled with subtly toned cushions, and the walls—the walls were a positive
feast of the most extraordinarily luminous
paintings she'd ever set eyes on.

'You seem surprised at the way this room
looks.'

Araminta spun round, nearly tripping on the
edge of the Arraiolo rug, then swallowed in
amazement as her eyes met a pair of dark,
slightly amused ones. The man who had come
in through the door that linked the drawing
room to the study next door stood six feet tall.
His jet-black hair was streaked with grey at the

temples, and his features—well, his features were positively patrician.

'I hope it is admiration and not disgust that has you eyeing this room so critically,' he said, raising a quizzical brow and giving her the once-over. Then he moved forward and reached out his hand. 'I am Victor Santander.'

'Araminta Dampierre,' she murmured, pulling herself together with a jolt. 'And, no, I wasn't being critical at all—simply marvelling that Sir Edward's dull drawing room could be transformed into something as wonderful as this.'

'It pleases you?'

His hand held hers a second longer than necessary. Surprised at the tingling sensation coursing up her arm, Araminta withdrew her hand quickly.

'Yes. It's—well, it's so unexpected, and bright, and so—well, so un-English. Yet it doesn't look out of place,' she ended lamely, hoping she hadn't sounded rude. It was bad enough that she'd bashed the man's car without insulting him as well.

'Thank you. I'll take that as a compliment. I think it brightens the old place up. I hope I haven't gone overboard with the Latin

American art, though,' he said, tilting his head and studying her.

'Oh, no,' she reassured him, eyeing the amazing pictures once more. 'That's what makes it utterly unique.'

Then, remembering why she was here, she drew herself up, wishing now that she'd worn something more flattering than her old jeans and sweater. Not that it mattered a damn, of course. But seeing him standing there looking so sure of himself, so irritatingly cool and suave in perfectly cut beige corduroy trousers, his shirt and cravat topped by a pale yellow cashmere jersey, did leave her wishing she had been more selective.

'I must apologise again for my careless be- haviour yesterday. I'm really very sorry to have caused your car damage.'

'It is not important.' He waved his hand dis- missively. 'Please, won't you take off your jacket and sit down? Manuel will bring us cof- fee.' He turned to the manservant hovering in the doorway and murmured something in a language she didn't understand. The man re- sponded by stepping forward and taking her jacket, before disappearing once more.

'Please. Sit down.' He indicated one of the large couches. 'You say that we are neighbours? I remember seeing a reference on the land map to Taverstock Hall. Does it belong to you and your husband?' Victor asked, taking in the gracefully tall woman standing before him, with her huge blue eyes, perfect complexion and long blonde hair cascading over the shoulders of an oversized sweater that did not allow for much appreciation of her figure. Quite a beauty, his new neighbour, even if she was careless.

'Uh, no. It belongs to my mother.' He watched her sink among the cushions, elegant despite the casualness of her attire, and sat opposite. 'As I said, I feel dreadful about yesterday. Still, I brought my insurance papers so that we can get it cleared up as soon as possible. Oh!' she exclaimed, her expression suddenly stricken. 'I put them in the pocket of my jacket.'

'Manuel will bring them. Never mind the papers,' he dismissed.

'Thank you.'

He eyed her up and down speculatively, and drawled, 'Frankly, I'm rather glad you banged into my bumper. I might otherwise never have had the opportunity of meeting my neighbour.'

He smiled at her, an amused, lazy smile, and again Araminta felt taken aback at how impressively good-looking he was. She also got the impression that she was being slowly and carefully undressed.

'Well, that's very gracious of you,' she countered, sitting up straighter and shifting her gaze as Manuel reappeared, with a large tray holding a steaming glass and silver coffee pot, cups, and a dish with tiny biscuits.

'Ah, here comes Manuel with the *cafèzinho*.' He smiled again, showing a row of perfect white teeth. 'In my country we drink this all day.'

'Your country?' She had detected a slight accent but couldn't identify it.

'I'm Brazilian. In Brazil we drink tiny cups of extremely strong coffee all day. This coffee you are about to drink was brought from my own plantation,' he added with a touch of pride. 'If you like it I shall give you some to take home with you.'

'That's very kind,' Araminta murmured, slightly overwhelmed by her handsome host's authoritative manner.

She watched as he poured the thick black coffee into two cups before handing her one. Then, as she reached for the saucer, their fingers touched again, and that same tingling sensation—something akin to an electrical charge—coursed through her. Araminta drew quickly back, almost spilling the coffee.

'I hope you are not a decaf drinker,' he said, his voice smooth but his eyes letting her know he was aware of what she'd just experienced.

'Oh, no. I love coffee. It's delicious,' she assured him, taking a sip of the strong brew, its rich scent filling her nostrils.

'Good. Then Manuel will send you home with a packet of Santander coffee.'

'That's most generous. Now, about the insurance,' she said, laying her cup carefully in the saucer, determined to keep on track and not be distracted by this man's powerful aura. 'Perhaps we should go ahead and—'

'I don't mean to be impolite,' he replied, looking at her, his expression amused, 'but do we have to keep talking about a dented bumper? It is, after all, a matter of little importance in the bigger scheme of things. Tell me rather about yourself—who you are and what you do.'

Araminta, unused to being talked to in such a direct manner, felt suddenly uncomfortable. His gaze seemed to penetrate her being, divesting her of the shroud of self-protection that she'd erected after Peter's death. It seemed suddenly to have disappeared, leaving her open and vulnerable to this man's predatory gaze.

'There's nothing much to tell,' she said quickly. 'I live at the Hall and I write children's books.'

'You're a writer? How fascinating.'

'Not at all,' she responded coolly. 'It's a job, that's all, and I enjoy it. Now, I really feel, Mr Santander, that we should get on with the car insurance. I need to get to the village; I have a lot to do this morning,' she insisted, glancing at her watch, feeling it was high time to put a stop to this strange, disconcerting conversation.

He looked at her intensely for a moment, then he relaxed, smiled, and shrugged. 'Very well. I shall ask Manuel to bring your jacket.'

'Uh, yes—thanks. It was silly of me to leave the papers in the pocket.'

'Not at all,' he replied smoothly. 'You are a writer. Creative people are naturally distracted because they live a large part of their existence in their stories.'

Araminta looked up, surprised at his perception, and smiled despite herself. 'How do you know that?'

'I know because I have a lot to do with artists.' He waved towards the walls. 'Most of these paintings are painted by artists who are my friends. I am a lover of the arts, and therefore have a lot to do with such people. They are brilliant, but none of them can be expected ever to know where their keys are to be found. I am never surprised when I arrive at one of their homes and the electricity has been cut off because someone forgot to pay the bill!'

He laughed, a rich, deep laugh that left her swallowing. And to her embarrassment, when their eyes met once more Araminta felt a jolt at the implicit understanding she read there.

Unable to contain the growing bubble inside her—a mixture of amusement at his perception and embarrassed complicity—she broke into a peal of tinkling laughter. And as she did so she realised, shocked, that she hadn't laughed like this for several years. Not since the last time she and Peter—

She must stop thinking like that—not asso-
ciate everything in her life with her marriage.

'You obviously have a clear vision of what
artists are like,' she responded, smiling at
Manuel as he handed her the jacket.

She removed the papers from her capacious
pocket, careful not to spill her worldly belong-
ings: keys, wallet, dog leash, a carrot for
Rania, her mare, and a couple of sugar lumps.
She caught him eyeing the wilting insurance
documents and blushed. 'I'm afraid they're a
bit crushed, I've had them in my pocket a
while.'

'As long as they're valid, it's of no importance.'

'Right.' Araminta pretended to concentrate
on the contents of the documents, but found it
hard to do so when he got up and came over
to the couch, then sat casually on the arm and
peered over her shoulder as though he'd
known her a while. Araminta caught a whiff
of musky male cologne. 'Here, Mr Santander,'
she said, shifting hastily to the next cushion.
'Take a look at them. Perhaps we should
phone the company?'

'Why don't you leave these with me?' he
said, taking the documents from her and glanc-

ing over them briefly. 'I'll deal with this matter. And, by the way, since we're neighbours and not in our dotage, perhaps we could call each other by our Christian names?' He raised a thick, dark autocratic brow.

'Yes, I suppose so,' she replied nonchalantly, trying hard to look as if meetings of this nature happened to her every day. Then quickly she got up. 'I think I'd better be going. Thanks for the coffee, and for being so understanding about the accident.'

'De nada,' he answered, rising. 'Allow me to help you with your jacket.'

Another unprecedented shudder caught her unawares as his hands grazed her shoulders when he slipped the jacket over them.

'It has been a pleasure to meet you, Araminta.' He bowed, and to her utter surprise raised her hand to his lips. 'I shall phone you once I know more regarding the insurance.'

'Yes, please do.' She smiled nervously and began moving towards the door. The sooner she escaped the better.

Victor followed her into the hall, then after a brief goodbye Araminta hurried down the front steps, a sigh of relief escaping her as she finally slipped onto the worn seat of the Land Rover and set off down the drive.

What on earth was the matter with her? she wondered. And what was it about this man that had left her feeling so bothered, yet so unequivocally attracted?

Which was ridiculous, she chided herself. She wasn't interested in men any more, knew perfectly well that she would never meet another man like Peter as long as she lived. Dear, gentle Peter, with his floppy blond hair, his gentle eyes and charming English manners. Even her mother had liked Peter, which was saying a lot.

Of course he hadn't been terribly capable, or prudent with their money, and had made some rather unwise investments in companies that his friends had convinced him were a really good idea and that had turned out to be quite the opposite. But that didn't matter any more—after all, it was only money.

The fact that because of his carelessness she was now obliged to live with her mother at Taverstock Hall she chose to ignore. Death had a funny way of expunging the errors and accentuating the broader emotional elements of the past.

*   *   *

Victor Santander walked back into the drawing room of Chippenham Manor and stared at the place on the couch where Araminta had sat. She had come as a complete surprise. An agreeable one, he had to admit. He couldn't remember a time when he'd taken any pleasure in talking to a woman he barely knew.

Oh, there were the occasional dinners in Rio, Paris and New York, that ended in the suite of his hotel, with high-flyers who knew the name of the game. But ever since Isabella had taken him for the ride of his life he'd lost all trust in the opposite sex. So why, he wondered, when he, a cynic, knew perfectly well that all women were wily, unscrupulous creatures, only out for what they could get, had he found Araminta's company strangely refreshing? He'd even taken her insurance papers as an excuse to get in touch with her again. And she'd seemed oddly reticent—something else he was unused to—as though she wasn't comfortable being close to a man.

The whole thing was intriguing. Not that he was here to be intrigued, or to waste his time flirting with rural neighbours. He'd come to the English countryside to seek peace of mind, make sure his horses were properly trained and take the necessary time to study his latest business ventures without interruption.

Still, Araminta, with her deep blue eyes, her silky blonde hair and—despite the shapeless sweater—he'd be willing to swear her very attractive figure, had brightened his day.

With a sigh and a shake of the head Victor returned to the study, and, banishing Araminta from his mind, concentrated on matters at hand.

CHAPTER THREE

'Two hundred thousand copies!' Araminta exclaimed, disbelieving. 'Surely that can't be right? You mean they like my new book that much?'

'Yes,' her agent, Pearce Huntingdon, replied excitedly down the line. 'They're talking about television interviews and the works. It's going to be a raving success. Get ready for the big time!'

'But I don't know that I want the big time. I mean, of course I do want my books to be a success, for children to enjoy them and all that, and perhaps make some money too. But not all the hype the—'

'Rubbish. You'll love it.'

'No, I won't,' she replied firmly. 'And I don't want you making any publicity arrangements on my behalf without consulting me first, Pearce. I'm just not up to that sort of thing yet.'

There was a short silence. 'Araminta, when are you going to let go the past and face the fact that you have a brilliant future ahead of you? I know you started writing as a hobby, as something to get your mind off all that had happened. But it's time you took yourself and your career seriously. *Phoebe Milk and the Magician's Promise* is a wonderful, captivating book that every child in this country is going to adore if it's marketed right. For goodness' sake, woman, wake up and smell the coffee.'

The reference to coffee caused Araminta to remember Victor Santander's flashing black eyes, and then to glance over at the gold and black packet of freshly ground coffee sitting on the kitchen counter. He'd had it delivered later in the day.

'Look, let's talk about this once we know it's real,' she countered, not wanting to argue with Pearce, who could be terribly persuasive when he wanted. 'I'll think about it and be in touch.'

'All right, but don't think too long. I'm not letting you miss the chance of a lifetime because you're determined to wallow in the past.'

'Pearce, that's a cruel thing to say,' Araminta exclaimed crossly.

'No, it's not. It's the truth. And the sooner you face it the better.'

'Oh, shut up,' she muttered, smiling, knowing he meant well.

But as she hung up the kitchen phone Araminta noted that for the first time in months she felt extraordinarily exhilarated. Her book looked as if it might take off, and, despite her desire to banish him from her brain, she could not help but recall her new neighbour's captivating smile, and the musky scent of his aftershave as he'd leaned over her shoulder to look at her car insurance papers.

How absurd. She was reacting like a teenager to a handsome face. She must stop, she admonished herself, glancing at her watch and realising it was nearly time for tea. There was no room in her life for anything except her writing and getting out from under her mother's roof. The rest—a social life, friends, a man and all that—would just have to wait for a time in some remote future that she tried not to think too much about.

'Was he perfectly dreadful?' Lady Drusilla enquired as soon as Araminta brought in the tea tray.

'Who? The new neighbour?'

'Well, of course the new neighbour. I would hardly want to know about the new milkman,' Lady Drusilla muttered disparagingly. 'I wish you would be less dreadfully vague, Araminta, it's a most annoying trait. I would have thought you'd have grown out of it by now.'

Counting to twenty, Araminta placed the tray down on the ottoman and reminded herself that if all went well, if the book really did take off, she might not have to stand her mother's jibes for too much longer.

'Well?' Lady Drusilla prodded. 'What was he like?'

'Oh, all right,' Araminta replied evasively.

'What do you mean, all right? Is he young? Old? Handsome? Rich? Or just dreadfully common? One of these *nouveau* yuppie types?'

'Frankly, Mother, he was very nice. He was most gracious about the fact that I mucked up his car and that it'll have to go into the repair shop, and, no, he was not common in the least. Quite the opposite, in fact. I thought he was very much the gentleman. He gave me a packet of his coffee.'

'Coffee?' Lady Drusilla raised an astonished brow. 'You mean he's a food merchant?'

'Not at all. He is—among, I would imagine, a number of other things—the owner of a coffee plantation in Brazil.'

'Oh, well, that's rather different, of course.'

'I don't see why,' Araminta answered crossly. 'Frankly, I couldn't give a damn what the man does. The main thing is he seems to be quite pleasant and will hopefully be a good neighbour. He's Brazilian, by the way.'

'Well! I never thought to see a Brazilian coffee-planter at the Hall. Poor Sir Edward must be turning in his grave. Why that dreadful cousin of his didn't keep the place, I can't imagine.'

'Thank goodness he didn't. One look at him was enough to let me know he would be the kind of neighbour we could do without.'

'Mmm. You're right, I suppose. He wasn't very prepossessing, was he?'

'No, Mother, he wasn't. And I can assure you that Victor Santander is far removed from Henry Bathwaite. Plus he speaks perfect English. I should think he was probably brought up here.'

'Perhaps he had an English mother—or maybe a nanny,' Lady Drusilla mused. 'Do be careful pouring, Araminta, I've told you a hundred times to use the strainer properly.' Lady Drusilla let out a long-suffering sigh. 'You are aware that I have to chair the committee for the Hunt Ball this evening, and that I shall require your help, aren't you?'

'Mother, I'm sorry, but I simply don't have the time. I have to finish the proofs of my book.'

Lady Drusilla pursed her lips. 'I find it quite incredible that you should abandon your true responsibilities because of some ridiculous children's story. I thought I'd brought you up better than that.'

Araminta was about to tell her mother about the two hundred thousand copies her publisher was putting on the market, and the launch party being planned, but thought better of it. The less her mother knew about her burgeoning career the better. At least she wouldn't be able to put a spoke in the wheel. So she contained herself with difficulty and remained silent. Perhaps it would even be worth doing some of the public appearances, however hateful, if it meant she could buy her freedom and finally be her own person.

Three days later, Lady Drusilla had just picked up her basket to go and collect some vegetables from the garden when the phone rang.

'Hello?' she said, glancing out of the window, annoyed at being interrupted when she was sure it was about to rain.

'Good morning. Could I speak to Miss Dampierre, please?'

'*Mrs* Dampierre. I'm afraid she's out. Who would like to speak to her?'

'This is Victor Santander.'

'Ah. The new neighbour. I am Lady Drusilla Taverstock, Araminta's mother.'

'How do you do, Lady Drusilla? I haven't yet had the pleasure of your acquaintance, but I'm hoping that may be remedied in the very near future.'

Lady Drusilla unbent. At least the man had good manners. 'How do you do? Perhaps you'd better come over to dinner some time?'

'That would be very kind.'

Lady Drusilla thought quickly. She simply must get him over here before Marion Nethersmith caught him first. Then she could tell the others all about him. 'What about to-morrow night?'

'It would be my pleasure.'

'Good. I'll expect you at seven-thirty for drinks.'

'Thank you. Perhaps you could tell your daughter that I shall bring her car insurance papers back to her then?'

'Certainly.'

'I look forward to tomorrow.'

Well, Lady Drusilla, thought as she picked up the basket once more and headed for the backstairs and the kitchen, where she removed her secateurs from the top drawer, at least she'd steal a march on the other neighbours. Marion would be writhing with curiosity and envy.

The thought brought her a considerable measure of satisfaction.

'You did what?' Araminta exclaimed, horrified, hands on the hips of her other pair of worn jeans.

'I invited him over to dinner. Araminta, are you becoming hard of hearing?'

'But, Mother, how could you? We don't even know the man properly. It's embarrass-ing—' She threw her hands up in despair.

'I really can't see why you're making such a dreadful fuss. I merely invited our new neighbour—whom you say is perfectly re-spectable—to dinner. It's the courteous thing to do.'

'I can't believe it. You didn't even ask me if I wanted—' Eyes flashing, Araminta flopped into the nearest armchair, trying to understand why the thought of Victor Santander coming to dinner should be so absolutely disturbing.

After being told by Araminta that Victor Santander had uniformed servants at the Manor, Lady Drusilla decided to call in the local caterer, Jane Cavendish, and have dinner properly prepared, rather than count on Olive's rather dull repertoire of dishes. That would do for old Colonel and Mrs Rathbone, but would certainly not impress someone grand enough to hire a professional cook.

By seven-fifteen the following evening Araminta's bed was piled with discarded cloth-ing as she wavered between a black Armani sheath that she'd bought shortly before Peter died and had never worn, or grey silk trousers and a top.

Perhaps the sheath was too dressy for a simple dinner.

Perhaps the grey silk was too dull.

After changing for the third time, she finally settled on the silk trousers and top, and after a last glance in the mirror—she'd actually gone to the trouble of putting on some make-up tonight, for some unfathomable reason—she walked down the wide staircase, feeling more confident than she had in months.

Perhaps it was time to bother more about her appearance, she decided, reaching the bottom step, particularly if she was going to have to promote herself. The thought made her shudder as she made her way to the drawing room, where her mother was giving last-minute instructions to the hired help. With a sigh, she went to join her.

Even in the dark, and illuminated only by the car lamps and outdoor lights, Taverstock Hall was an imposing old pile, Victor reflected as the Bentley purred to a halt. He alighted thoughtfully, straightened the jacket of his double-breasted dark grey suit, and walked smartly up the front steps and rang the bell. It was opened by a cheery-looking woman in what could be taken for a uniform, and he was ushered through the high-ceilinged hall and on towards the drawing room, from which voices and the clink of crystal drifted.

On the threshold he stopped a moment and took in the scene. Then he saw Araminta. For thirty seconds he enjoyed the view. His intuition had been right, and her figure was as sensational as he'd imagined it. She was stunning—and deliciously sexy, he realised, watching her as she stood sideways, talking to an old gentleman near the open fireplace. Long and lithe, the curve of her breast subtly etched under the sleeveless silk top— His thoughts were abruptly interrupted.

'Ah, Mr Santander, I believe?' A very distinguished, rake-thin woman in her mid-sixties, dressed in a smart black cocktail dress with a large diamond leaf pinned on her left breast, moved towards him. He raised her hand to his lips.

'Good evening, Lady Drusilla, it is most good of you to have me.'

'Not at all. Thank you so much for the lovely flowers. Quite unnecessary, I assure you,' she murmured, taking in every detail of his person. 'Now, do come in and meet the others. You've met Araminta, of course, and this is Colonel Rathbone and Mrs Rathbone—they live not far down the road, at the old vicarage—and this is Miss Blackworth.' He shook hands politely with an elderly lady in a nondescript purple dress and a three-tier string of pearls before turning to meet what must be the vicar. 'Vicar, may I introduce Mr Santander? Our new neighbour at the Manor.'

Her tone of satisfaction was not lost on Victor and he glanced at her, amused. So Lady Drusilla was enjoying introducing him into local society, was she? At that moment he raised his eyes and met Araminta's. They held a moment, and he read amusement laced with discomfort and a touch of embarrassment. After exchanging a few words with the balding vicar, he edged his way towards her.

'Good evening.'

'Good evening,' she replied, smiling politely, disguising her racing pulse, the slight film of perspiration that had formed on her brow the minute she'd sensed he'd entered the room. 'I hope you won't be too bored. The country doesn't provide much in the line of entertainment, I'm afraid.'

'I did not come to the country to seek entertainment,' he replied, his presence and the scent of that same cologne leaving Araminta deliciously dizzy. 'In fact, I came here specifically to find peace and quiet. I did not expect to be invited out so soon,' he added. 'Still, it is, of course, a great pleasure to meet one's neighbours. Particularly when they are so...agreeable.' He gave her an appraising look that left her feeling strangely feminine and desirable, something she hadn't felt in ages.

'What can I get you to drink?' she said quickly.

'A Scotch and water, please.'

Glad for the excuse to conceal her perturbed feelings, Araminta busied herself with the drink. What on earth was wrong with her? He wasn't anything special. Just a neighbour.

Victor watched as she fixed his drink. A beautiful woman with tons of sex appeal. She probably had a husband. He wondered where that husband was. Odd that she seemed so shy for a married woman. Or maybe she was recently divorced. That might explain the reticence.

The thought was strangely appealing. Then with an inner shrug he accepted the drink and prepared to amuse himself for an evening.

From the opposite end of the table Araminta watched her mother grilling Victor Santander and admired his polite, concise answers that gave little away. But, oh, what she would have given for this evening not to have taken place! By the time coffee had been drunk, after-dinner drinks consumed and the better part of the guests had taken their leave, she was only too ready to usher him out through the door and send him off to his car.

'This has been a most pleasant evening,' he remarked, eyeing her again in that same as-sessing manner that left her slightly breathless. 'Could I persuade you to join me for dinner tomorrow at the Manor? After all, we haven't had a moment to go over the insurance pa-pers.'

'No, we haven't,' Araminta admitted, fum-bling for words. It was very unlike her to be so—so what? Aware of herself? Of him, stand-ing so close that it left her feeling tingly all over? What on earth was wrong with her?

'Well? Would you like that? Or would you prefer to dine at the Bells in Sheringdon? I hear they serve a very decent meal.'

'I don't think I can,' she said hurriedly, seeing her mother hovering in the hall. 'Why don't we speak tomorrow and set up a convenient time to do the papers?'

'As you wish.' He pressed his lips to her hand. Then, to her amazement, he brushed his lips on the inside of her wrist.

Araminta withheld a gasp as a shaft of molten heat coursed from her head to her abdomen. With a gulp she snatched her hand away, caught the devilish gleam in his eyes and the amused smile hovering at his lips, and seethed inwardly at her silly reaction. Then he moved, lean and predatory, towards the car.

Heart thudding, Araminta watched the Bentley purr smoothly off down the drive, then turned with a sigh of relief and stepped inside. This was ridiculous. How could she be put in a state because a man touched her hand? Thank God she'd refused Victor Santander's offer of dinner if this was the way he affected her.

She never felt stirrings for any of the men she knew, yet for some inexplicable reason this

Brazilian—who was almost a stranger—had touched something deep within her that she'd believed gone for ever. It both frightened and excited her. Her instinct warned her that the less she saw of the man the better. She knew very little of him, but sensed there was something sophisticated and dangerous about him. He was, she told herself firmly, the last person she would want to get involved with. That was if she was thinking of getting involved with anyone—which, of course, she wasn't.

'Araminta?'

'Yes, Mother, I'm coming.' Araminta closed the large front door, then made her way back through the hall to the drawing room, where her mother was seated complacently by the fire, twiddling a final glass of champagne.

'Well, I must say that I was most favourably surprised by our new neighbour. Did you know that he went to Eton?'

'No, I didn't. Mother, if you don't mind, I think I'll go up to bed,' she said, passing a hand over her brow. 'I've a bit of a headache.'

Lady Drusilla, dying to assess the evening further, pursed her lips in annoyance. 'Oh, very well,' she muttered.

And Araminta made good her escape.

CHAPTER FOUR

A COUPLE of days later Araminta told herself that any passing attraction she might have felt for her new neighbour was nothing more than that. She'd kept busy, going over and over the proofs of her book, making sure any last-minute errors did not escape her before she sent back the final version to her editor who was having it published at record speed. But today she was taking a break, and going riding.

As she gave Rania her head and galloped across the Downs, Araminta enjoyed the cool wind in her hair and the sense of freedom that was so far removed from being cooped up in the house, bent over her laptop, as she had been for the past days. But at least the proofs were ready and she could post them off to-morrow.

Slowing her pace, Araminta became aware of another horse and rider coming out of the copse. She glanced in their direction, noting the equestrian's good seat and the fine propor-tions of the horse. Then all at once her heart stood still and she gulped. Surely it couldn't be Victor Santander?

She'd been so involved in her work for the past few days that she'd forgotten the phone message he'd left and the insurance that still needed to be dealt with. Now, as the horses approached one another, she braced herself. He would probably be cross that she hadn't phoned back. And he'd be entitled.

Victor reined in the fine chestnut and watched appreciatively as Araminta brought her mount to a stop. She looked quite lovely astride the skittish mare. A flash of amusement gripped him as he approached, realising that her expression was that of a guilty child. Amused rather than annoyed that she had obviously forgotten all about his call, he reined in next to her. The truth was, it intrigued him to meet a woman who was so outwardly unresponsive to him, yet who he was certain held hidden depths of sexual response.

Suddenly the idea of setting out to seduce Araminta and find out if that response truly existed became vastly appealing. He'd discovered now that she was a widow. Good. No jealous husband to contend with. Plus, he'd never seduced a widow. This could be a first.

'Hello,' he said casually, riding alongside her now, noting how lovely she looked, her cheeks pink and her golden hair a windblown mass that he wished he could drag his fingers through.

'Hello.'

'You didn't get my message?' he asked, looking her straight in the eye, allowing her no escape, amused as the colour in her cheeks heightened. He smiled inwardly. It would definitely be amusing to see the fair Araminta Dampierre writhing to his touch. And writhe she would, he assured himself, with all the arrogant confidence of one used to getting his own way.

'I'm afraid I forgot to phone back,' she apologised. 'I've been very busy with my book the past few days.'

'I see,' he responded coolly. 'Well, I got in touch with the insurance company and they'll be sending you some forms to complete.'

'I'm sorry. I should have remembered.'

'Yes, you should.'

'Look, I don't know what to say.' She bit her lip and reined in the horse. 'I really am sorry. I get a bit carried away when I'm working.'

'Hmm.' He eyed her carefully, wondering if she was ready. Like the mare she was restraining, she would need careful handling, this one, he reflected, taking her measure. It surprised him, but she obviously had little experience of handling men. Or being handled.

'Is there anything I can do to make up for having put you to all this trouble?' she asked doubtfully.

'Actually, there is,' he said, a smile hovering now he knew he'd got her where he wanted.

'Tell me—what?'

'Have dinner with me tonight.'

'Oh, I don't think—'

'You said you wanted to make up for having put me to so much trouble,' he reasoned, a sardonic gleam in his flashing golden-flecked dark eyes.

'Yes, but—'

'But?' He raised a quizzical brow. 'Is having dinner with me such a penance?'

'Of course not. All right,' she conceded, smiling and giving in. 'What time?'

'Eight o'clock at the Manor. Though I can pick you up, if you'd prefer?'

'Oh, no. I can pop over.'

'Then, *à toute à l'heure*,' he said in French before glancing at the sky. 'You'd better get home before it pours. I'll race you to the road.' He turned his horse and set off across the Downs.

Never able to refuse a challenge, Araminta raced after him. Soon they were riding neck and neck in an exhilarating dash across the Sussex countryside and arrived simultaneously at the roadside.

'We seem to be pretty well matched,' he said, eyeing her admiringly as they pulled up at the crossroads.

'That was fun!' Araminta exclaimed, laughing engagingly.

'We must make sure we repeat the exercise,' he agreed, leaning over and taking her gloved hand in his, seeking her eyes. 'I shall await you at eight.'

Then he wheeled the horse around and cantered off in the direction of the Manor, leaving Araminta wondering why on earth she had accepted what she knew to be a dangerous invitation that must surely spell trouble. She would do well to keep their conversation on neutral ground, she realised, grimacing as the first drops of rain fell. This man was by far too smooth, too knowing, and the increasing attraction she was experiencing was ridiculous, to put it mildly. Instinctively she sensed that she was out of her league. But surely she could control this silly attraction? Surely that couldn't be too hard?

Turning her horse, she headed for home, telling herself that all it took was self-discipline. Nothing more.

He was standing far too close for comfort, and his whole being was far too overpowering, Araminta realised as she listened to his knowledgeable analysis of several paintings gracing the drawing room walls. Araminta showed suitable interest, wondering all the while how it was possible that a man she barely knew could have such a powerful effect on her.

It was as if she'd changed, as if something within her yearned for him in a visceral, primitive way that was not only unladylike, but which she'd also always despised in other women. The truth was she'd never experienced such longing first-hand. In fact, now that she thought about it, she'd rarely been just physically attracted to anyone. Even when she'd met Peter it had taken quite a while before she'd realised she was fond of him. And that had been because of his character, his charm, his fun, not because he oozed charisma and sex appeal.

But this man was different. Even as they chatted he exuded a tense, dangerous quality that should repel but that instead acted upon her like a magnet.

Dinner was delicious—lobster bisque followed by roast pheasant. Victor had gone to great trouble to make her feel at ease. To her astonishment Araminta confided in him, told him about her next book, and some of her future hopes and fears in that domain. And he listened, obviously interested and admiring.

She sighed now, feeling warm and at ease. Perhaps it was a combination of the pleasant conversation, the softly candlelit room, the wine and the after-dinner drink that she held loosely in her left hand that were responsible for her being so aware of him. She smiled when he looked down at her, those dark eyes flecked with gold so penetrating that she wondered suddenly if he could read her soul. She shivered and hoped he hadn't a clue what was on her mind. Wished she didn't know herself.

'Are you cold?' he asked, slipping a firm arm around her shoulder and turning her slowly towards him.

'No, I'm fine,' she murmured, aware that her pulse was beating wildly, willing herself to move away from him. But her body didn't follow her head.

'Let me take your glass.' Victor laid it down on the small table next to him, his eyes mesmerising hers. Jazz played softly in the background, and for a moment Araminta wondered if this was real or merely a dream from which she would suddenly wake.

Then Victor took a step closer, and she could feel the warmth of his body, breathe the scent of his aftershave. For a moment a flash of logic penetrated the delicious haze surrounding her, telling her this was asking for trouble. But his hypnotic gaze was upon her, she could feel his body heat, could not resist the draw as his arms slipped possessively around her. And all at once Araminta knew that, defying all reason, she wanted his kiss more than anything.

And it came. Surprisingly soft at first, then harder, his tongue exploring her mouth in a manner so new and so unknown, so different from anything she'd experienced with Peter that she almost drew back. For this was no quick, purposeful kiss designed to prepare the way for what was to follow, but rather a slow, lazy, languorous, delicious, yet taunting discovery.

Even as the kiss deepened, Araminta knew that she had never experienced anything similar before, and slowly she gave way to the myriad of sensations coursing through her being, felt her body yield, soft and melting in his arms, felt his hardness against her and knew that she had never desired a man as she desired Victor Santander.

His hands were wandering now, travelling up and down her spine, along her ribcage, cupping her bottom, bringing her even closer, caressing, pressing her to him, until, oblivious to reality, she let out a sigh of utter longing.

The next thing she knew they were lying on one of the wide couches and Victor was deftly unbuttoning her silk blouse. Even as her brain told her she should put a stop to this immediately, her body craved his touch and she could do nothing to halt the onslaught. When his thumb grazed her nipple through the thin texture of her bra she gasped, and a shaft of heat, a white hot arrow like none she'd ever known, left her arching, yearning for the touch of his fingers, travelling south, deftly removing all barriers, seeking until he encountered the soft mound of throbbing desire between her thighs. When he cupped her she let out a moan of delight and threw her head back, unable to do more than succumb to the delicious torture, give way to the turmoil of sensation that exploded in a pent-up rush when his fingers finally reached her core.

'You are beautiful,' he whispered, 'gorgeous, and I want you.'

As Araminta lay in his arms, recovering from the most unexpected, mind-shattering orgasm of her life, a tiny voice spoke in the back of her mind. This couldn't be happening, shouldn't be happening. Was she really lying wantonly with Victor Santander—a man she barely knew—allowing him to touch her intimately? What must he think of her?

In fact, at that very instant he was determinedly trying to strip her of the rest of her garments.

With a jerk Araminta pulled herself up and out of his arms.

Victor fell back and looked at her, brows creased. 'Is something the matter, *querida*?' he asked, dragging his fingers through his thick black hair, eyes bright with undisguised desire.

'No—yes—look, I don't know what happened just now,' she mumbled hoarsely, aware of her mussed hair as she fumbled around for her bra and shirt. 'I—I know this will sound absurd, but I honestly don't know how it happened.'

She began fiddling with the hook of her bra, then the buttons of her blouse, wishing she were a thousand miles away, feeling her cheeks burning as all at once she realised just how far this whole episode had gone. And so quickly. It was unthinkable, shaming, even ludicrous that she could have behaved in such a manner with a total stranger.

Victor rose from the couch and, picking up his brandy snifter, stood a few feet away, watching her thoughtfully. He made no attempt to hold her back, merely contemplated her feeble attempts to tidy herself as though he were a spectator at a show. What had happened to make her react thus? he wondered. For, despite his initial spark of anger at her sudden rejection, his interest was piqued.

He considered himself a pretty good judge of character, and her sudden willingness to succumb to his caresses had surprised him. Now, as he stood there in the aftermath of their tryst, he reflected that his first opinion of her— that she was relatively inexperienced and unaware of just how attractive and sexy she was—was probably the correct one. Well, then, perhaps it was better that things hadn't gone any further.

He walked to the window, letting himself cool down while Araminta sorted herself out. Better, he repeated silently. Still, he could not pretend that what had just happened between them hadn't been incredibly seductive and to his utter surprise, incredibly unique. Okay, it was just a kiss and a few caresses but— Victor cut off the thoughts that followed and turned.

'Why don't you stay the night?' he asked, suddenly but smoothly, unwilling to let her go.

'I—look, this never should have happened—never has happened before. I don't know how it did,' Araminta mumbled, embarrassed.

'It happened because we both wanted it to happen,' he said harshly, viewing her through

narrowed eyes. 'Because we are two consent-
ing adults who feel desire for one another.'

'Perhaps,' she conceded grudgingly, retriev-
ing her shoe from beneath a cushion. 'But that
isn't a reason to—well, to—' She threw up her
hands.

'To go to bed together?' he finished. 'Why
on earth not? I can't think of any better reason.'

'Can't you?' she exclaimed, suddenly cross.

'Well, I can. Tons of them.'

'It took you rather a long time to remember
them, *querida*,' he murmured dryly.

Araminta steadied her gaze and he read anger there. 'Perhaps it did. I don't know where
my head was at. I'm sorry if I misled you. I
had no intention of giving you the wrong impression. I—look, I need to go home.'

'Why of course,' he murmured with a sardonic twist of his lips. He watched her pick up
her purse, ignoring a sudden twinge of disappointment. Though why he should feel disappointment when he barely knew this woman
was ridiculous!

Perhaps it was proof that, despite all he'd
been through with Isabella, he still hadn't
tamed that irrationally romantic nature of his.

Or was Araminta Dampierre less innocent than she seemed? He of all people knew what women were capable of. Why, for a single moment, should he imagine that this one might be any different from all the others?

As she drove down the dark country road and headed back to Taverstock Hall Araminta took herself seriously to task, asking over and over how she could possibly have behaved in such a wanton manner. Never had anything remotely similar occurred before in her life, not even when she was a teenager. That Victor was a man whom she'd met only a few times didn't make it any better. And thank goodness for that sudden flash of common sense that had intervened just in time, or right now she might very well be rolling between Victor Santander's wretched sheets!

It was appalling, shocking, and so unlike her that she had difficulty recognizing herself in the writhing woman of minutes earlier. For a moment she thought of Peter, and a new wave of guilt swept over her. She hadn't thought of him once all evening, hadn't remembered the gentle, quiet nights spent in each other's arms after tender but, she had to admit, guiltily comparing the sensations of earlier in the evening, not very exciting sex.

Araminta changed gears crossly as she swerved into the gates of Taverstock Hall. That she should suddenly be denigrating her marriage was as absurd as all the rest. She'd been happy, hadn't she? Had never felt that what they'd had was less than enough, had she? So why this? Why now? Why had she soared to unknown heights at the touch of a near-stranger, and never during the entire course of her sedate marriage to a man she knew—was one hundred per cent certain—that she had loved? Surely there must be something seriously wrong with her?

Too troubled to go straight into the house, and possibly have to face her mother, Araminta dropped her car keys into her pocket and wandered into the rose garden, where she sat down on one of the stone benches. With a sigh she stared up at the half moon flickering through fast-travelling cloud and tried to make sense of the evening. But whichever way she viewed it she still couldn't come up with any justification for her strange behaviour. She must, she concluded, have lost her mind. And she'd better make damn sure it never happened again. Not paying attention while parking, she reflected grimly, could carry a high price.

Victor was also too wound up to go to bed, and he stood for a long time by the window, wondering why she'd allowed him to go that far. Was she innocent, or a hypocrite? he pondered, wishing to banish the niggling feeling of frustration that still hovered. Whatever, it was probably a lot better that she had upped and left when she had, for otherwise it might have proved embarrassing to have her wake up next to him when he'd had no intention of anything more than a night of good, satisfying sex.

In fact, all round it was definitely preferable this way, he persuaded himself, wandering back to the drawing room and absently pouring another cognac, before retiring to the study to do some work before going up to bed.

But half an hour later he found it impossible to concentrate on the project at hand. He must be tired, he concluded, folding up the plans of a new factory in Brazil.

'Damn Araminta,' he exclaimed, banishing the image of her lovely face as she'd reached orgasm in his arms, and the strangely satisfying sensation he'd experienced when he'd heard that little gasp of surprised shock that told him quite clearly she'd never reached those heights before.

With a sigh and a short harsh laugh directed at himself, Victor downed the last of his brandy. Then, switching off the lights, he headed upstairs to bed, determined to rid his mind of his fair neighbour.

CHAPTER FIVE

THERE was no use pretending it hadn't happened, Araminta realised the next day. She just had to face the fact that for a few inexplicable minutes she must have gone mad.

As it happened she was given little opportunity to stew over the events of the night before, for early in the day the telephone rang.

'Araminta, it's Pearce. Look, they're advancing the book-launch date and there's a huge party planned at the Ritz. I can't believe it—they're going to have it published in record time,' he said excitedly.

'Oh. Will I be expected to be there?'

'Well, of course you will, silly girl. You're the one person who has to be there, come hell or high water.'

'But I don't think I—'

'One more word and I'll scream,' Pearce roared down the phone. 'Araminta, get with the programme! This is *your* book, *your* success. Don't you feel the least bit excited about it all? Girl, you're about to make millions if it flies!'

'Really? Yes, I suppose I might,' she muttered vaguely. The thought of being exposed to all those strangers, having to smile and chitchat, sound intelligent and answer questions about her book was thoroughly daunting.

'Araminta, it's not the end of the world,' Pearce continued patiently. 'You used to be so social before you married Peter. What's the matter with you?'

'Oh, I don't know. I've changed, I suppose.'

'Not really. You're just hiding.'

'Peter didn't like going out much, so we rarely did.'

'Araminta, Peter is no longer with us,' Pearce said carefully. 'And you are. You have to make a life for yourself. Thanks to your own efforts you're going to be a great success. Enjoy it, girl, instead of running away.'

'I'll think about,' she murmured, twisting the cord of the telephone. 'When is the party going to be?'

'In three weeks.' He gave her the date.

'So soon?' Araminta squeaked.

'Yes. Goodness knows how they're getting the books done in time. And you'd better get yourself to London and buy a decent dress for the occasion. Don't think you can come in those worn jeans of yours. I won't have it. I want you to look stunning. In fact I'll go shopping with you if need be.'

'That won't be necessary,' Araminta responded in a dignified tone. This was all happening far too fast. First last night, now this. It was as if she couldn't stem the flow of events sweeping her along, despite her desire to stay cushioned from the world at Taverstock Hall.

But as she hung up she heard her mother calling from the stairs and winced, closing her eyes. Perhaps this really was her chance to move on. Of course if she moved it would mean more change. But at least she'd have a choice, which at present she didn't. Plus, it would mean she wouldn't be stuck next door to Victor Santander.

This last did more to get her moving than any other element of the equation. The mere thought of coming across him in the village or elsewhere was enough to cause a rush of hot embarrassment. What would she do? How would she face him if it happened?

'Araminta, I really must have your help for the Hunt Ball,' Lady Drusilla said, walking into the hall and bringing her crashing back to earth.

'I'm sorry, Mother, but I'm afraid I'll be away at that time,' she responded absently.

'Away?'

'I'm going to London. I have to do some stuff for my book. There's going to be some sort of launch party on the same day as the Ball.'

'Goodness. How very tiresome.' Lady Drusilla pulled her cardigan closer and sniffed. 'Couldn't you have got your publishers to arrange it another day? It can't be *that* important, surely?'

'Actually, it is,' Araminta replied, drawing herself up suddenly aware for the first time just what she was about to achieve. 'They're publishing two hundred thousand copies.'

'Goodness. That seems rather excessive, doesn't it?' Lady Drusilla's brows rose in disapproval. 'I hope they won't sit on the shelves. It could be a terrible waste of good paper.'

Furious at her mother's response, Araminta turned on her heel and decided that Pearce was right. She needed out, needed to get on with her life and not tolerate her mother's impossible behaviour any longer. In fact, she decided, running up the stairs and dashing the tears from her cheeks, the sooner she went to London and began looking for something decent to wear for the party the better. After all, if she was going to be the centre of attention then she might as well do it right.

Three weeks later Araminta stood in the ballroom of the Ritz surrounded by Pearce, her publishers, and a number of journalists, critics and miscellaneous celebrities brought in for the occasion. There were stands with copies of *Phoebe Milk and the Magician's Promise* tastefully placed about the room, waiters circulated with trays of champagne and elegant finger food, and a jazz quartet played at the far end of the room.

For a moment Araminta blinked, and wondered if the blend of soft music, the clink of fine crystal, laughter, extravagant compliments and conversation was real. She caught a glimpse of herself in one of the mirrors and felt an adrenaline rush, knowing she looked really good in the Dolce & Gabbana cocktail dress, with her hair beautifully washed and blow-dried by one of London's top hairdressers. It made her feel confident, more able to deal with the hype surrounding the launch and her own role in all this.

Then all at once, as she turned to answer a question put to her by a trendy-looking journalist with spiky hair and little round glasses, she froze. Surely that couldn't be Victor Santander standing across the room by the double doors, in a dark navy blue jacket and grey trousers, looking her over appreciatively?

Glancing quickly away, she tried desperately to calm her racing heart and concentrate on what the young journalist was saying. But her eyes kept wandering. Her tummy lurched and she swallowed nervously, gripping the stem of her champagne flute for dear life. How had he known? What on earth could he possibly be doing here?

Victor Santander watched her from his position near the door and smiled to himself. So he'd been right to come after all. When his old friend Pearce Huntingdon had commented over lunch at White's, their club, that tonight he had the launch of a big book that was going to hit the top of the lists, Victor had asked who the author was. When Pearce had mentioned Araminta's name Victor had pricked up his ears and directed the conversation so that the unsuspecting Pearce had ended up inviting him to come along.

Now, as he watched her from across the ballroom, Victor felt that same smouldering rush of attraction. She looked very different from the way he'd seen her in the country, deliciously chic and sophisticated in a dress that subtly accentuated each curve of her slim, sensuous figure. He wasn't quite sure why he had come. Perhaps the memory of that same lithe body writhing in his arms had stuck in his mind, despite his determination not to let it linger there.

Realising that she'd seen him, he made a beeline across the room to where she stood, allowing her no room for escape.

'Good evening—and congratulations,' he said, coming smoothly alongside, so that she was sandwiched between him and the keen-looking journalist.

'Good evening.'

'Quite a do, this. Your book looks as if it's going to be a big hit.'

'Hmm. Thanks.'

'Hmm? Is that all you have to say?' He quirked an amused brow.

'Well, what do you expect me to say? ''Yes, I'm going to be a number one bestseller''?' she asked crossly.

'Now, now, *querida*, don't get upset,' he murmured, reading the confusion in her eyes and deciding to put her at ease. Perhaps the other night had been an aberration after all. 'I'm sure you've heard all sorts of exaggerated compliments all evening and have had about enough.'

Slightly mollified, Araminta met his eyes and read the humour there. 'As a matter of fact you're right,' she replied ruefully. 'Plus, I'm not used to wearing high heels and my feet are killing me.'

Victor grinned, took quick stock of the room, saw that guests were beginning to trickle out, and made a quick decision. 'You know, we could probably slip away without being noticed and go somewhere for dinner. You could kick your shoes off under the table.'

'I can't leave my own party,' she said, tempted by his offer. The strain of having to smile and be bright all evening was beginning to weigh on her. 'And, by the way, tell me, what are you doing here?'

'I was invited,' he said, with the devastating smile that, Araminta noticed with irritation, already had several women peering in their direction.

'By whom?' she asked coolly.

'By Pearce.'

'Pearce?' she exclaimed. 'How on earth do you know Pearce?'

'We were at Eton together. We happened to lunch today at White's, and he mentioned your name and the launch. I then made it my business to cadge an invite.' His eyes were filled with bold, arrogant laughter, and despite the lingering embarrassment Araminta smiled.

'Come on,' he encouraged, his voice cajoling, 'be a devil. You've done your bit for the book. You don't have to stay till the last guest leaves.'

'Pearce will kill me.'

'Don't worry about Pearce. He'll do as he's told. I was his prefect.'

She looked at him and laughed again. 'You can be very bossy, can't you?'

'So I'm told. But it serves its purpose.'

'And what might that be?' she asked, realising with shock that she was flirting with him.

'That remains to be seen.' He looped his arm through hers and glided discreetly towards the side door to their left. 'Don't look too obvious about it. We'll just slip into the hall as though we were going for a breath of air.'

'I need to fetch my coat.'

'You can get it from the cloakroom tomorrow.'

'But I'll freeze to death. It's—'

'I'll keep you warm, don't worry.'

'I really think—'

'Araminta, just shut up and do as you're told,' he ordered, grabbing her hand as they crossed the lobby of the hotel. 'My car is waiting.'

As they stepped outside Araminta saw the Bentley drawn up on the kerb. A chauffeur jumped out and quickly opened the door. Next thing she knew they were driving down Piccadilly, and Victor had his arm around her and was rubbing her shoulders, not in a seductive way, but in a warm, practical manner.

Several minutes later they drew up in front of Annabel's, a nightclub in Berkeley Square.

As she was freshening up in the Ladies' Araminta thought about the strange course the evening had taken. Surely she must be mad to be here with Victor Santander, the one man she'd been determined to avoid for the past few weeks, had cringed from every time she turned a corner in the village in case she came across him.

But tonight she felt strangely exhilarated. The enthusiasm about her book was real, the press was talking about it, and tomorrow it would be on the shelves. She hoped it would sell as they believed it was going to. It would be too awful if after all this hype it was a flop. She felt a sudden rush of anxiety, then banished it. She might as well enjoy the evening. Whatever else he was, Victor was intelligent, amusing and good company. But tonight she would make sure that she made it back to Pont Street and her friend Sara's flat in one piece, and not allow herself to be sidetracked along the way.

With a determined nod she closed her evening purse and, smiling to the attendant, entered the club.

*   *   *

She was truly lovely, Victor realised as the head waiter settled them at their table and he ordered champagne. Lovely, intelligent and successful. An interesting combination, he mused. He had taken time to observe her as she'd circulated among the guests at the party, observing her poised elegance, her gracious smile—very different from the slightly shy, retiring person she'd given the impression of being before. Intriguing. He wondered now how she was feeling after the excitement of the evening.

As Victor rarely thought about women's feelings at all—or certainly hadn't since the disastrous events in Rio that had burned him more than he liked to remember—he was surprised at his own reaction.

'Shall we dance?' he asked, after they'd finished dinner and their coffee, and were sipping champagne again.

He noted a wary gleam enter Araminta's eyes. 'A truce, Araminta. I am not going to try and seduce you. It's only a dance.'

'Okay.'

They rose and joined the other couples on the dance floor, swaying to the soft Latin rhythm. As his strong arms encircled her,

Araminta experienced a frisson—that same dangerously delicious sensation she'd known when he'd touched her before—reminding of just where and how that touch had ended. A tiny sigh escaped her and damp heat melted inside. But she ignored it, determined to enjoy the moment, the music, and the delightful atmosphere, not to hanker after the impossible.

It was ages since she'd been to a club—not since before her marriage, she realised wistfully, for Peter had hated nightclubs and would never come. Tonight took her back to the days when she'd been a girl about town, spending long, amusing evenings with her friends, visiting different fashionable hot spots. But all of that had come to an abrupt end when she'd married and moved to the country.

Victor proved to be an excellent dancer, moving her smoothly about the floor, and she let herself go with the rhythm, enjoying it as she never would have believed possible. He was amusing and friendly all evening, never mentioning their previous encounter, obviously determined to put it behind them and her at ease. But, as though to thwart all logic, she experienced an irritating stab of disappointment.

Perhaps all he'd wanted that night at the Manor was a not-too-bad-looking, conveniently available female. Then another thought occurred and she wondered suddenly if his seemingly bland attitude wasn't a ruse, a way of making her feel comfortable so that he could pounce again when she least expected him to.

This last thought made her laugh inwardly. She wasn't a mouse, was she? She was quite capable of making up her own mind about what she wanted and didn't want to do. It was just a matter of being firm.

The music ended and they returned to their table to sip more of the deliciously crisp champagne. Victor seemed suddenly thoughtful, and she took a sidelong look at his handsome tanned profile, wondering what he was thinking about.

'I have a proposition to put to you,' he said at last, turning on the banquette and looking directly at her through those golden-flecked eyes that, despite her decision to remain indifferent, left her feeling deliciously vulnerable.

'Oh?' A slight flutter of her heart made her swallow. What was he about to suggest?

'I am leaving the day after tomorrow for Normandy. I have a place there, and horses that are being trained. I'd like you to come with me.'

Araminta took a long sip of champagne. 'I don't think that will be possible.'

'And why not? I'm not asking you to sleep with me, but to come as a friend. No ties, just a few days' R&R. My plane is ready.'

'I don't think I should go,' she responded. 'I don't think it would be suitable. Plus, I have don't have enough clothes here, and anyway I need to get back home.'

'To what? To your mother and the aftermath of the Hunt Ball, *querida*?' He quirked a mocking brow at her that told her he knew exactly what was going on back home. 'I would have thought you could use a break from all that.'

The truth of this could not be denied. Still, she knew she was on dangerous ground. Victor Santander was too smooth an operator to be taken at his word.

'It's very kind of you to ask me,' she replied, sounding prissy to her own ears. 'It's just—'

'It's not kind in the least,' he interrupted. 'I like your company. This is not a ploy to seduce you,' he added, his lips twisting in a cynical curve. 'After all, I think you'll agree that what occurred the other night occurred by mutual consent.'

'I—'

'Stop being embarrassed about something perfectly natural that we both enjoyed. What happened happened. It's in the past. Forget it. We can start over as friends. Truly, I'd enjoy your company,' he said in a softer voice, slipping his hand over hers.

'What about my coat at the Ritz?' she said lamely, trying to think of an excuse, and wondering what her mother would say if she knew her daughter was thinking of flying off to France in a private jet with a man of whom she knew very little.

This last thought decided her. She'd had enough of following Lady Drusilla's dictates. And, although she hated to admit it, Victor was right. She needed a break. So why not take the opportunity and go?

'All right. I'll do it,' she said suddenly, flashing him a big smile, astounded at her own daring. 'I can use tomorrow to shop for a few more clothes and things.'

'Good. Then we'd better get moving,' he replied with a satisfied smile, and signalled the waiter.

CHAPTER SIX

THE Gulfstream landed at Deauville airport, and soon Araminta and Victor were whizzing through the Normandy countryside in a shiny Aston Martin, headed towards Falaise, the historic town still dominated by the centuries-old castle where that William was born who later set out in 1066 to conquer England. It was raining fairly hard by the time they drew up at a delightful eighteenth-century millhouse, just below the castle walls.

'How lovely!' she exclaimed, as Victor drew into the courtyard.

'I'm glad you approve,' he remarked, bringing the car to a standstill. 'I've had this place for a couple of years now, but I don't come here very frequently.' He didn't add that he'd bought the property just before Isabella had performed her stunt, and that coming here somehow reminded him of the whole disastrous affair.

But today it seemed different.

Araminta's presence, her obvious delight at the place and her straightforward manner, made it possible to relegate the negative thoughts that he associated with Isabella to the nether regions of his brain and concentrate on the present.

As they approached the front door it opened and a middle-aged woman in a skirt and twin-set appeared with a broad smile.

'*Bonjour, Monsieur Victor,*' she exclaimed, smiling at Araminta while taking the bags from him. '*Bienvenue.* It is so good to see you back here.'

'Hello, Madame Blanc, it's good to see you too.'

'How long does *monsieur* plan to stay?' she asked, leading the way up a wide stone staircase of shallow steps above which hung a delightful chandelier—an old-fashioned bronze balloon with candleholders.

'A few days,' he replied, his tone non-committal. 'You can put Madame Dampierre's things in the turret room,' he added, standing aside for Araminta to enter the large drawing room.

It was very English and different in style from the Manor, with pink walls and classical paintings, and wide velvet armchairs and comfortable sofas before the huge open fireplace where a fire crackled merrily.

'It's delightful!' Araminta exclaimed, moving towards the hearth, stretching her hands out towards the flames. 'I'm surprised you don't spend more time here.'

'Are you?' He looked at her hard, then joined her by the fire. 'I suppose I could. I have my horses at another property of mine, not far from here.'

'So you keep horses here and in Sussex?' she probed.

'Yes. I used to—'

He cut off, staring into the flames, and for a minute she wondered where he was. He seemed far away, as though remembering another time, another place. But she didn't push him.

'What about a drink?' Victor asked, snapping back to the present, then stepping towards a large silver tray weighed down with crystal tumblers and decanters.

'I'd love one.'

'Then I'll open a bottle of champagne. Just wait here and I'll be back in a second.' With that he disappeared down a small flight of stairs that must lead to the dining room and kitchen.

With a sigh of contentment Araminta sank into one of the enveloping armchairs, glad she'd taken the bull by the horns and come. It was relaxing to be somewhere so quiet and welcoming. Not that Taverstock Hall wasn't quiet, she reflected, but the thought that at any moment her mother might pop into the room and make some unexpected and usually negative comment always left her tense.

Now that she was away, in a place far removed from her family home, she was able to put into perspective just how negative her mother's continuing criticism actually was. She sighed and looked out at the rain pattering on the windowpanes, thinking how good it felt to be ensconced in this lovely warm room, with no stress, no obligations, and no one to accuse her of making mistakes.

'There was a bottle of Cristal on ice,' Victor remarked, coming back up the steps holding it.

He looked so good, in faded jeans and a black polo neck sweater, the sleeves of which he had pulled up so that she could observe the way the muscles of his tanned forearms tensed as he worked on uncorking the bottle.

Araminta swallowed and looked away, reminding herself that she had consented to come here just as a friend, and hastily turned her thoughts to the champagne. It was only a quarter to twelve, but somehow it seemed appropriate. As he handed her a flute she smiled at him. In fact, ever since the plane had left the ground she'd felt an inner smile bubbling inside her.

'To your success,' he said, raising his glass, his eyes firmly upon her. 'May *Phoebe Milk and the Magician's Promise* be at the top of the bestseller list. I love the title, by the way.'

'Thank you,' she responded sincerely. For it was true that now that she'd faced the possibility of success it tasted sweeter than she'd anticipated. And meant that she'd finally be able to escape Taverstock Hall, possibly find a home of her own again. Not that she knew where that home would be.

'A penny for your thoughts?' he said, sitting on the sofa opposite and stretching his long legs out towards the fire.

'Oh, nothing much.'

'Come on, tell me. I don't bite.'

No, Araminta thought wryly, you kiss. And rather well. But she was determined not to allow thoughts like that to penetrate.

'I was thinking that if everything goes according to plan I might be able to buy myself a home,' she remarked taking a long, delicious sip of champagne.

'Are you planning to move away from Sussex?'

'I have no idea yet.' She shrugged. 'It's just a thought.'

'What would your mother have to say?' he asked, his tone deliberately bland, his eyes focused on the contents of his glass.

'I have no idea. But probably quite a lot.'

'She appreciates your company,' he observed shrewdly.

'No, not really. She likes having someone she knows is dependent upon her whom she can boss around.'

'And whom she can bully,' he supplied dryly.

Araminta looked up quickly. 'How do you know that?'

It was his turn to shrug. 'I'm a good judge of character, that's all. Your mother seems to have quite a strong nature, *querida*.'

'Domineering, you mean,' Araminta said with feeling. 'I suppose it's my own fault, for letting her have her way, but sometimes it's just easier than getting into an argument.'

'You don't like arguments?'

'I loathe and detest them. I like living in a harmonious atmosphere.'

'And was your marriage harmonious?' he asked quietly, shifting his position on the sofa to get a better look into her eyes.

'Yes—yes, it was. Very.'

'I see.'

The tone of his voice made it seem as though 'harmonious' and 'quiet' were uninteresting.

'It wasn't dull,' she added quickly.

'I never said it was.'

'It was— Well, it was...' She tried desperately to think of a word that would define her marriage to Peter without sounding negative.

'Boring?' he supplied, his gaze direct.

'Not all,' she answered, a little too quickly. 'Of course it wasn't boring. It was nice and pleasant and—'

'Predictable?' he pressed.

'Yes. And I don't see what's wrong with that,' she replied defensively.

'Nobody said anything was,' he countered reasonably. 'Now, why don't you take that champagne upstairs with you and see if you approve of your room? It's in the turret.'

'Good idea,' she responded, relieved to bring this uncomfortable conversation to an end.

'I'll see you back down here in half an hour for a refill, as they say in America, and then we'll have some lunch.'

'Lovely.' Araminta smiled brightly and followed him down the tiny flight of stairs to the dining room, then through to the turret and its spiral staircase.

'Why, it's delightful!' she exclaimed, enchanted, gazing at the four-poster bed and the toile de Jouy curtains and hangings.

'I'm glad you approve.' Before she could move into the room he raised her hand to his lips, turned it over, and kissed the inside of her wrist. 'May you be happy here, *querida*.'

Before she could answer he was gone.

Araminta looked about her, delighted by the charm of the place, the peace, and the intoxicatingly heady feeling of being alone and away from the world, with this devastatingly attractive man, and in such a magical spot.

Now, Araminta, she admonished herself. *You mustn't lose your focus. You came for a few days' relaxation, nothing more.*

On that philosophical note, and despite the fact that she knew she might very well be trying to deceive herself, Araminta opened her bag and began unpacking, glad that she'd bought a couple of warm garments in London, as it looked as if it might get quite chilly. She sighed and smiled and began hanging things in the wonderful lavender-scented oak armoire. She really didn't want to think any more than necessary right now. Soaking up the atmosphere and letting go of tension was all that really mattered.

After a delicious lunch of *boeuf à la bourguignonne* and a bottle of Château Haut Brion, an exceptional cheese platter and some amusing conversation, Araminta and Victor sat once more in the drawing room, where Madame Blanc brought in a tray piled with steaming coffee and chocolates.

'I hope you don't plan to have meals like this for the whole length of our stay,' Araminta exclaimed.

'Why not? Didn't you like it?' Victor frowned.

'Quite the contrary.' Araminta laughed. 'Everything was simply delicious, but I dread to think of the weight I'll put on.'

His face softened and he smiled. 'I doubt you need to worry about your weight. In fact it might not do you any harm to fill out a bit. You're very slim.'

'And plan to remain so,' she said meaningfully.

'Why is it women are obsessed about being thin when we men actually prefer you with a bit of quantity as well as quality?'

'That sounds dangerously familiar,' Araminta mused.

'It was what Spencer Tracy used to say regarding Katharine Hepburn—that quality was all fine and dandy, but what about some quantity?'

Araminta's shoulders shook with laughter.

'Don't laugh,' he continued, handing her a cup of coffee, eyes sparking wickedly. 'It's nice to have something to feel.'

'Hmm. I'm sure,' Araminta responded and, knowing they were getting onto dangerous ground, hastily changed the subject. 'Are your horses far from here?'

'Not very. About twenty minutes. Would you like to see them?'

'I'd love to.'

'Very well, then we shall go and take a look at them tomorrow morning. I thought this afternoon we might drive into Deauville. There's not much going on at this time of year, but still, some of the shops are open.'

'That would be lovely,' she responded, quite happy to fall in with any plan. 'I think it's stopped raining.'

'Perhaps for a little while, but Normandy is like England—renowned for the rain. So take a raincoat and an umbrella.'

'Okay, I will. What time would you like to leave?'

'In about half an hour?' His eyes rested on her for a moment.

'Fine.' Araminta jumped up, his intense gaze making that familiar tingling sensation return. 'I'd better go upstairs, then.'

'I'll see you in the hall when you're ready.'

He stood up as she left the room and watched as she disappeared down the short flight of stairs.

It was strange to have a female guest in this house. He hadn't brought anyone since his marriage to Isabella had collapsed. In fact the thought that he'd actually bought the house for Isabella, when all the while she was two-timing him with another man, still had the power to arouse his anger. But not like it used to. Those days were over. Gone, thank God. He would always despise her, but he didn't hate her any longer. She simply wasn't worth it. What he could never forgive her for was the child she'd been carrying, that she'd aborted so as not to have any further attachment to him. That he would never forgive.

Ever.

Victor stared out of the long French window at the lush green grass and the lawn beyond. He wasn't a man who craved a child, but the thought that any woman could cold-bloodedly kill his offspring was horrifying to him.

Turning slowly, he gazed once more into the flames and thought of Araminta. What had driven him to go to her party and then bring her here? She was a lovely woman—one who, in the few moments she'd spent in his arms, had touched some long-forgotten chord deep within him. But it would be ridiculous, of course, to let anything reach beyond the well-erected walls that for the past couple of years he'd made sure were in place around his emotions.

For a moment he continued to stare into the flames, and wondered if Araminta really believed that they were only here as friends or if she recognised the deep magnetic attraction pulling between them. He sighed, and turning again, looked up through the other window at the castle.

Women were strange creatures; they seemed to take pleasure in deluding themselves. Why couldn't she just take this trip for what it would inevitably turn out to be? A few delightful days consummating their burning desire for one another. Once that was over they could both return to their everyday lives, none the worse for wear. But neither did he plan to rush things. Araminta was not an experienced woman of the world. She'd been married, but he had a good idea what kind of a marriage it had been.

An enigmatic smile touched his lips as he turned back and faced the room. He wasn't in any hurry. In fact, taking his own lazy time would make it all the more amusing.

*   *   *

Two hours later they were walking along the windswept seafront at Deauville, past the restaurants that in summer were packed with tourists and habitués, past the famous hotels and the casino, and along the deserted windblown beach. There was no one else about, except a man with a dog and two elderly ladies.

As they faced the wind Araminta experienced a rush of exhilarating well-being. Victor slipped an arm through hers and they walked for a while in companionable silence, enjoying the bracing fresh air, the fast-traveling cloud.

Then Victor put a friendly arm around her shoulders, and Araminta knew she could not resist the tug, the insatiable desire that had consumed her ever since that first evening at the Manor. Was it not absurd to resist it? she asked herself suddenly, slowing their pace and looking out to sea.

As though sensing her change of mood, Victor turned her towards him and gazed down into her eyes.

'Why deny ourselves when we both want the exact same thing?' he queried, his voice carried on the wind.

A smile touched her lips. 'Why, indeed? Kiss me, Victor. I've decided I want to be kissed.'

'Your wishes are my commands,' he answered promptly. And his mouth closed on hers, strong and demanding, making her gasp with delight as once more her being melted, molten gold pouring into a mould of his making.

After several minutes locked in each other's arms he looked up. 'Let's go home,' he murmured roughly.

'Let's,' she agreed, taking his outstretched hand and running with him along the seafront in carefree delight.

All at once she felt light, liberated, as though all the cares of the world had been lifted and at last she could breathe. For an instant she wondered what the consequences of it all would be. Then, shunning logic, she laughed up at him, determined to enjoy the journey, wherever it led.

An hour later they were back at Le Moulin. There was no time for niceties, no time to do more than make it up the winding turret stairs before Victor ripped off her shirt and, throwing her on the four-poster, proceeded to devour her.

Never in her wildest dreams had Araminta imagined that lovemaking could be like this—hot, wanting, tempestuous and wild. Her hair splayed over the pillows, the sheets; she writhed in his arms, unable to control the shafts of searing heat and need crashing through her. The feel of his skin on hers and the sound of his husky voice whispering words in a tongue she did not understand left her dizzy as never before.

Next morning she woke from a delicious sleep to the feel of something soft gently caressing her hair. She kept her eyes closed and enjoyed the sensation, still half asleep and not quite conscious yet of where she was. Then all at once she opened her eyes and gazed, amazed, into Victor's handsome face looking down at her.

'Good morning,' he murmured. 'I brought you a cup of coffee.'

'Oh, thanks.' Araminta struggled to sit up, but he slid a hand onto her shoulder and she recalled the events of the previous afternoon and evening.

They had only left the bedroom to concoct Victor's superb omelettes and share a bottle of *premier cru* Château Latour, before returning to their nest in the turret. Now, in the harsh daylight, Araminta blushed at the things she herself had initiated, had felt uninhibited enough to do with a man she barely knew.

'No. Stay like that,' he ordered, his hand slipping to her cheek and down her throat as she reached for her dressing gown.

His eyes were intense and Araminta drew in her breath. Was she going to allow this man to dictate the time and place by a mere look? Be at his beck and call whenever he decided he wanted her?

There was no use denying that the intense attraction existed—no use pretending they both didn't want to consummate their relationship again, in the light of day now peeking through the toile de Jouy curtains.

But before she could think further Victor had slipped his hand below the duvet. His eyes dark with desire, he grazed her taut nipple, making her gasp. Then, before she could protest, his mouth was on hers, his lips prying hers open.

For a moment she tried to draw back, but he merely laughed. Then the firm, unyielding insistence of his tongue working its way cunningly into her mouth left her clutching his hard shoulders once more as he drew her into his arms, pressing his hand into the small of her back, moulding her bottom. Her taut breasts pressed hard against his chest as he moved onto the bed. His tongue probed further now, thrusting, leading her to a wild, untamed response. She could feel his renewed desire to possess her, knew she was ready for more— knew that once he'd decided she could not, would not, resist.

Victor took it slowly this time around, sensing her waning resistance, determined to make her follow her instinct and her soul. Then, smoothly and firmly, he moved on top of her until she could feel the length of him, until her tongue sought his as passionately as his sought hers. And, just as it had the previous night, there came a point when Victor knew that he too had lost control.

All at once he heard her moan, and the sound made him groan. In one swift movement he pulled back, leaving her naked before him. She was beautiful, sensual, all woman, he reflected, before kissing her throat, her breasts—those wonderful pink-tipped breasts that betrayed her every feeling as his tongue flicked and taunted them—and she arched, crying, begging him to satisfy her deepest desires.

There was no use resisting, Araminta realised. She could do no more than throw her head back and moan, giving herself up entirely to his expert caresses. He kissed further down, down, until his tongue finally reached her core, laving, taunting, causing such excruciating pleasure that she let out a gasp of sheer delight and surprise.

No man had ever done that.

All at once she relished in the joy, the spiralling tension rising within as she dragged her fingers through his thick black hair, pleading with him to bring her to completion.

But still he lingered.

It was only when she thought she could bear it no longer that he slipped his other hand from behind her and, fondling her breast, worked on her with his tongue, bringing her to a peak in a searing wet rush of heat so intense that she cried out, begging for fulfilment and release. Then, just as she could bear it no longer, as her nails dug into his broad shoulders and she was ready to beg for mercy, the hot intensity that had built up crashed, let loose, and she floated into an incredible ecstatic joyride that prolonged itself on and on, until she fell back among the crumpled sheets limp and weak, yet knowing she wanted what she knew was to follow.

'Minha linda,' Victor whispered, gazing at her before he sat up and slipped off his robe, and joined her again in the bed. Araminta extended a hand and touched his thigh.

'Victor, what is happening between us?' she whispered, dazed. 'Why is this so wonderful?'

'You've never felt like this before, have you?' he murmured, an edge of pride to his voice.

'No.' She shook her head. 'I haven't. I—I never knew it could be like this. Or reacted like this, for that matter,' she added, a faint blush tinting her cheeks.

He smiled down at her, his bronzed features etched in the morning light. 'We have only just begun, Araminta,' he said, leaning on his elbow and observing her.

'I know,' she whispered, with a little smile that curved her lips.

She was beautiful lying there, all woman, her long blonde hair splayed across the pillow, her body so sensual, so feminine and lovely, already well satisfied, yet ready, he sensed, to arch once more to his touch.

Slowly he let his fingers roam over her again, smiling as she shuddered. Her eyes sought his, read the question in them.

Then, knowing he could wait no longer, Victor moved on top of her, waited a second to read her reaction and, seeing her eyes dilate with expectation, thrust deep within her, needing to know her warmth, to feel himself sheathed in her soft, yielding being, to bring his arms around her, kiss her neck and delight in the feel of her legs wrapping around his waist as together they found a hard, fast, all-encompassing rhythm that sought and demanded, each drawing all they could from the other.

Somewhere through the haze that was his mind he heard her gasp, knew she was once more close to completion, and he plunged deeper, determined to reach the inner core of this woman he knew so little of but who, in a strange way, had given him something he'd believed lost for ever.

Then together they came in a rush of ecstasy, Victor throwing his head back and Araminta crying with joy as they exploded, then fell entwined among the sheets, unable to do more than bask in the aftermath of their lovemaking.

'Are you okay?' he whispered several minutes later, when he'd got back his breath and his pulse was beating at a normal pace once more.

'Yes,' she replied, turning her head on his deliciously damp shoulder and nuzzling closer. He pulled her to him, his arm possessively flung around her shoulders.

'This is all so strange—so unexpected. So...so...' She couldn't finish her sentence.

'I know, *querida*,' he answered carefully. Then, 'Does it matter? Why not just enjoy it?'

'Yes,' she answered, knowing that for now all she wanted was the feel of his body close to her, the grip of his arm around her shoulders and the knowledge that they were here, in this magical little world of their own, and could set the rules. For a time.

'We're supposed to go and see the horses this morning,' he said after several moments.

'Then why don't we?' Araminta shifted onto her elbows and grinned at him.

He was incredibly gorgeous lying there bronzed and taut against the white sheets, his hair ruffled, his face softer than she'd ever seen it before. His dark eyes held a new light. Gone was the slightly bored, cynical air, replaced by something intense that she couldn't define and that left her swallowing.

'Okay. Don't just lie there.' She laughed. 'Let's get up and go and see these famous horses of yours.'

She felt full of a new vital energy now—a desire to walk, to run, to get up and get out. She felt alive. It was intoxicating and wonderful, something she'd never experienced—and the sudden realisation that it was years since she'd felt so energised left her shocked. Hadn't she ever felt like this with Peter?

As though guessing her sudden guilt, Victor rose and slipped his arms around her. 'No memories, okay, *linda*? We are here, now, and that is all that matters. The past and the future can take care of themselves. All that matters is what we're experiencing together at this time. Don't spoil it.'

She looked up, feeling she understood exactly what he meant, and nodded, allowing him to slip his arms loosely around her waist. 'You're right,' she agreed. 'Here and now. I think I'll get into the shower.'

'I'll do the same, and see you downstairs in half an hour.'

Dropping a kiss on her mouth, he turned, picked up his dressing gown and slipped it on, then, patting her bottom, he turned her in the direction of the bathroom. 'Off you go, beautiful.'

Half an hour later Araminta was in the hall. She wore jeans and a pair of Wellington boots that Madame Blanc had produced from the cloakroom, which fitted her perfectly. Mercifully she'd brought her new Barbour jacket, and had shoved a scarf into the pocket in case it rained.

'You look wonderfully English,' Victor remarked as he came down the stairs smiling, hair still sleek and wet from the shower, his dark corduroys and sweater giving him a dangerous look as he reached the flagstoned hall and dropped a kiss on the tip of her nose. 'I'll get a jacket and we'll go. I thought we'd grab some lunch at one of the country inns I know.'

'It sounds great.'

In fact everything sounded great, Araminta realised, as though she were living in a dream from which she hoped she wouldn't wake up. At least not for a while.

As they got in the car she realised she hadn't phoned her mother. Then she banished the thought. She would ring the Hall at a time she knew her mother would be out and leave a message on the machine. That way nothing she said could spoil this perfect moment.

Soon they were driving down charming country roads, complete with hedgerows and green fields that reminded Araminta of southern England.

'It looks rather like Sussex, doesn't it?'

'Yes, it does.'

'Is that why you bought the Manor?' she asked, suddenly curious.

'In part,' he replied stiffly, seemingly unwilling to elaborate.

'I see.'

'No, you don't, but never mind.' He gave her a hard sidelong look. 'If I told you why I bought the Manor it would involve travelling down that memory lane where we decided not to go, *querida*.'

'Okay.' Araminta shrugged and agreed. He was probably right. They were, after all, living a fantasy. A fantasy with no past and no future. Why sully it? Something in his tone told her that whatever it was that had driven him to abandon this spot and buy the Manor was not pleasant. She wondered all at once if he was married, or had been married, and if so where his wife was and if he had any children. But there again she forced herself to keep quiet. They were here together, living this specific moment, weren't they?

And that was all that mattered.

Soon they were drawing up into the courtyard of a beautiful château. Several charming brick buildings surrounded the yard, the grass was beautifully kept and the gravel raked. In the distance she could see a small lake and an exquisite little château.

'It's delightful!' she exclaimed.

'You think so?'

'Of course it is. What an amazing place to keep your horses. I can't think why you don't stay here all the time instead of at the Manor.'

Victor made no response. His expression was dark for a moment, then he smiled and waved to a small bow-legged man hurrying towards them.

'*Bonjour*, Gaston. How are the horses doing?'

'Very well, Monsieur Victor. Very well indeed.'

'Good. Then perhaps we'll take a look at some of them.'

'Certainly. Shall I meet you at the stables?'

'Yes. We'll walk over there.'

Victor slipped Araminta's arm through his and they took a path leading through the trees towards the château. The gardens were beautifully laid out, swans glided gracefully on the lake, and the scent of autumn filled the air.

'Is this property yours?' she asked, suddenly frowning.

'It belonged to my mother. She died three years ago.'

'I'm sorry.'

'I inherited it, and I keep most of my horses here.'

'But the house looks so beautiful,' she exclaimed, gazing across the lake at the château, exquisite in design and size, not too big.

'It is a lovely place. I spent time here as a child. Maybe some day I'll redo the house and—' He cut himself off abruptly, then turned down another path. 'Let's get to the stables before it rains again. It certainly looks as if there will be another downpour, *querida*.'

Since he obviously didn't want to talk about it, Araminta decided not to ask him more. But she concluded there must have been some strong motive for Victor first to have acquired Le Moulin and then the Manor in Sussex. She reminded herself that it was none of her business. Yet, despite her determination to live only in the present moment, she couldn't help but feel curious about him and the rest of his life.

But when they reached the stables all thoughts and conjectures were forgotten as she became engrossed by the fine creatures being presented to them. Some of the horses were champions, or would probably become champions in the next few years. She loved the foals and spent some time stroking their silky coats.

An hour later they were driving into a village. Araminta exclaimed as they entered, for it was exactly what she'd imagined a Normandy settlement would look like: timbered cottages, with tiny windows and crooked roofs, and narrow cobbled streets.

Soon they were seated at a corner table in a delightful low-beamed restaurant, facing an open fireplace. Victor ordered a bottle of excellent red wine, but as they settled in, and Araminta studied the menu, she wondered suddenly what subjects, apart from general ones, they could talk about if the past and future were not to be mentioned.

It was strange how full, yet how empty, a single moment in time could be without those two elements. It left just them and their feelings. Nothing more. Like two ships that cross in the night, she reflected. And although that was enthralling, and made her recall this morning's delicious lovemaking, she could not stop wishing that the man beside her would reveal more about himself, what drove him, and what lay beneath that suave outer shell.

CHAPTER SEVEN

THE weather that evening turned colder, and after dinner Araminta and Victor sat together in each other's arms on the large sofa next to the fire. It seemed strangely natural to be curled up with him among the cushions, Araminta's head resting on the shoulder of Victor's soft cashmere sweater, sipping a cognac and reading her book while he flipped through the paper.

For a moment she experienced a sudden rush of longing for something more than the barren life she lived at present, for something involving warmth and affection and domesticity. She stopped herself with a sharp jolt at the word love, for it was simply too dangerous, too unreal to think of anything like that. Particularly when the man next to whom she was sitting had made it abundantly clear that they were merely living a few moments in time, that in a few days or hours they would come to an abrupt end.

A tiny sigh escaped her as she tried to concentrate on the subject matter of her book.

'What's the matter, *linda*?' Victor asked, bringing his arm closer around her shoulders and looking down at her. Araminta tilted her chin up and smiled. 'Nothing. I'm fine. Really enjoying myself. How about you?'

'I'm fine too,' he said, then turned to stare with a hooded gaze at the flames crackling in the grate. At that moment the telephone rang and, laying the paper on the huge ottoman before the fire, he rose to answer it in the hall.

Araminta heard him reply and tried to continue reading. But a sudden change in his tone made her look up and take heed.

'What do you mean, she's in trouble?' he demanded. There was a moment's silence, then, 'I see. I suppose you want me to come and deal with it, as usual? I thought by this stage I'd be through having to cope with more of her bloody nonsense.' Another pause. 'Okay. I'll fly out tomorrow.'

Araminta's heart gave a sharp lurch of disappointment. Whatever it was it wasn't good, and 'she', whoever she was, required his presence. This meant an immediate end to their magical time together. And despite her attempt not to let it trouble her she felt let down.

'I'm afraid I have some bad news,' Victor announced tersely as he returned to the fireplace, then stood drumming his fingers on the mantelpiece. 'I shall have to fly to Rio tomorrow, which means we'll have to curtail our visit here. I'm sorry.' His voice had become businesslike and harsh, and his expression was forbidding.

'I'm sorry too,' she replied, trying to keep the disappointment out of her voice. 'I hope it's nothing serious.'

He looked up then, as though seeing her for the first time. 'Serious? I don't know, exactly. Isabella has smashed her car into a bus and she's in hospital. Or so she says. Why they think I should have to go and deal with her is beyond me, but—'

'Isabella?'

'My wife,' he replied shortly.

The words hit Araminta like a ball of lead. She felt light-headed and swallowed, trying to regain her equilibrium and determined to suppress the knot forming in her throat. So he was married! She should have guessed. It had all been too good to be true.

'Are—are your children in Rio too?' she asked in a small voice.

'My children?' Victor frowned, a dark forbidding frown, and stared at her blankly.

'Yes. I presume that—'

'I don't have children,' he responded harshly, his features almost haggard now as he stared angrily into the flames.

Victor flexed his fingers, mastering his anger. Once again Isabella had imposed her unwelcome presence on him. And he resented her for it more than he could express. Isabella—the bane of his life. Why didn't her damn boyfriend see that she was properly taken care of? Maybe he was too busy sniffing cocaine.

'I need to make a couple of calls,' he said brusquely, 'then I suppose we'd better get to bed early. We'll leave here at seven sharp tomorrow morning.'

Turning abruptly on his heel, he left the room without so much as a sorry, or Would it be convenient?, or any of the things that any civilised normal person would have said.

Araminta's chest heaved with indignation. *He'd* omitted to mention he had a wife, so what right did he have to treat her in this dismissive manner now?

She let out some trapped air from her lungs, wrestling with her hurt feelings. Admittedly, it was partly her own fault. She'd come here by choice, without bothering to find out whether the man was married or not! And this was the result. That would teach her to be bowled over by a handsome face.

She was glad, she convinced herself, that they were to leave so early, for the sooner she got back to England and to reality the better it would be.

With an angry toss of her head, she picked up her book and, before Victor had a chance to return, headed upstairs to the turret, where, still seething, she prepared for bed.

After an hour of tossing and turning she fell into a troubled sleep, from which she was woken by a peremptory knock at five-thirty a.m.

'Breakfast in half an hour,' Victor's voice announced through the heavy oak door.

'Thank you,' she muttered, making a face at it.

Damn Victor Santander, his lies and his autocratic behaviour. Let him go back to his wretched wife. She just hoped that Isabella Santander was a complete pain in the neck. He deserved it!

Two hours later they were flying over the English Channel. Araminta sat in stony silence staring out of the window as the White Cliffs of Dover came into sight, unwilling to be drawn into conversation. Not that there was much conversation to be had, since Victor had spent the better part of the flight with his ear glued to his cellphone.

Soon the plane landed on the rainy tarmac, and Araminta experienced a wave of relief. Right now all she wanted was to get as far away from Victor Santander as possible—and preferably forget he existed.

Victor concentrated on two long telephone conversations that he could very well have made later in the day. Araminta was part of his life that he was putting on hold until he'd dealt with business back in Brazil.

'We can disembark now, Mr Santander,' the steward said politely.

'Very well. After you.' Victor nodded to Araminta, who picked up her large bag and marched ahead of him, head high, determined not to allow her inner turmoil to show.

In the airport, she was about to say she would rather take a cab when the same chauffeur who had driven them on the night of the party came forward and took her overnight bag. It would look silly and impolite to refuse the ride, so she walked smartly along next to a silent Victor and entered the vehicle, wondering why he was in such a foul mood. After all, it was he who had a wife, and it was Isabella who'd caused the trouble—not her!

By the time they reached Pont Street Araminta was only too thankful to be leaving his company.

Victor looked out of the window, then at her. 'Will you be all right?' he asked, making no move towards her.

'I'll be fine,' she answered in a chilly, haughty tone that left him in no doubt of her feelings.

'I'm sorry it worked out like this.'

'Never mind. It's probably for the best.' She sent him a bright, brittle smile that didn't reach her eyes and moved towards the door that the chauffeur was holding for her. 'Have a good trip.'

'I doubt I will. I'll call you when I return,' he added briefly.

The nerve of him! Araminta seethed, not bothering to answer as she alighted from the vehicle and made her way into the apartment block. The sheer nerve of the man! As she turned the key in the lock of the entrance door she watched the Bentley purr off into the traffic and let out an angry sigh. This would teach her to be more selective in the future.

Upstairs, she flung her bag next to the door and went to make herself a cup of coffee. Decaf espresso, she noted with satisfaction. She would throw that damn Santander coffee he'd given her into the bin the moment she got back to Taverstock Hall. She wanted no reminders of her stupid impulsive behaviour and its inevitable consequences.

Married, indeed. She should have guessed he was the kind of man who would be married and was just fooling around—should have sensed from the first day that he was the sort who probably kept his wife at home while he roamed the world and had affairs with different women. Only someone as pathetically naïve and stupid as herself would have fallen for his undeniable charm. It was shameful that she hadn't known any better.

As the kettle purred she drummed her foot nervously against a cupboard and glanced at the pile of forwarded letters Sara had left for her on the kitchen table. She noticed a list of urgent telephone calls to respond to as well. With a sigh, she picked it up. There was a message from her mother, and another from Pearce that read *'Very Urgent'*.

She sighed, peered at her watch, then waited for the kettle to boil before taking her mug of coffee and the biscuit tin through to the room with the telephone, aware that in her abstraction she hadn't even remembered to phone Pearce and find out how the first day of the book's sales had gone.

After a couple of sips she lifted the receiver, punched out his office number and was immediately put through.

'Araminta, where the hell have you been?' Pearce exploded righteously.

'Oh, just away,' she answered vaguely. The last person she wanted knowing her whereabouts was Pearce.

'How could you leave the party like that

without telling me? There were tons of people who wanted to meet you.'

'Oh, cool down, Pearce, it's not the end of the world. So, how have things been here?' she asked, nibbling at a ginger-snap.

'How have things been?' the irate Pearce squeaked down the phone. 'Things are fantastic, that's how things are. Record sales in the first two days. Of course the author wasn't available for comment,' he added, his voice laced with sarcasm. 'We could quite honestly say that we didn't know where she could be located.'

Araminta put down the biscuit. 'Did you say *record* sales?'

'Sold out lock, stock and barrel. They're printing another three hundred thousand copies as we speak. The kids are crazy about it—clamouring for books, lining the pavements in front of the bookstores, not to mention—'

'You're kidding,' she mumbled, flabbergasted.

'No, Araminta, I kid you not. I even had a telephone call from your wretched mother, who'd actually heard something on the news and wanted to know more, believe it or not.'

'Oh, God.'

'Is that all you have to say? *Oh, God?*

Surely after disappearing off the face of the planet for the past few days the least you could do is come up with something a little more imaginative—like, *Wow, Pearce, it's marvellous. You've done a great job?*'

'Pearce, don't be cross. I'm sorry,' she apologised, trying to assimilate all that was going on. 'It's just that— Look, I went away and something happened and I hadn't a clue about any of this. Are you free for lunch?'

'Of course,' he replied, mollified by her appeasing tone. 'I'll take you to Harry's Bar. Probably won't be left in peace anywhere else. By the way, are there any reporters outside Sara's flat?'

'I didn't see any.'

'Good. They were parked on the doorstep yesterday, but they've obviously realised you're not there. Perhaps it wasn't a bad thing you were away after all.'

'Pearce, do you really mean that *Phoebe Milk and the Magician's Promise* is a complete success? Not just us imagining it?'

'I'm telling you, girl, it's the real thing. You'll be looking to install yourself in a tax haven, you're going to make so much money. See you at one at Harry's.'

Araminta laid down the phone and tried to assimilate the twists her life had taken in the past few days. While she'd been away, acting like a starry-eyed teenager, she'd suddenly become famous. It seemed incredible, and she shook her head in bewilderment, kicking off her shoes and wishing Victor knew. It would serve him right. Though why she should care if he knew of her success or not when he was probably already boarding a flight to South America was beyond her.

Realising she'd have to get around to it some time, she lifted the phone again and called Taverstock Hall.

'Hello?' Lady Drusilla's imperious voice answered immediately. 'Ah, Araminta. Where on earth have you been? I've been besieged by the press, who seem to want to know all about you and this wretched book you've written. I've been feeling very off-colour lately. You really should have had some consideration for *me* when you decided to get into this profession. I've had who knows what kind of people ringing the front doorbell and asking all sorts of impertinent questions.'

'I'm sorry, Mother,' Araminta gritted, restraining her anger. Not even now that she'd succeeded, now that she was a success, had achieved what any other parent would have been proud of, could her mother think of anything but herself.

'When are you coming home?'

'I don't know,' she answered curtly.

'Well, what am I supposed to tell these creatures?'

'Oh, tell them whatever you like,' Araminta threw bitterly. 'How about, you have an ungrateful daughter who has no consideration for you or your comfort, and that frankly you'll be glad if she never steps foot over the threshold again?'

With tears running down her face Araminta slammed the phone down and threw herself among the sofa cushions, leaving Lady Drusilla holding the receiver in shocked astonishment.

Victor walked down the corridor of the private clinic in Leblon and knocked on the door of the room that had been indicated.

'Come in,' a soft feminine voice that he knew only too well responded.

'Hello, Isabella. I hope you're better,' he said without warmth, standing in the doorway observing her, his eyes narrowed. There seemed very little wrong with the woman lying there, beautifully attired in a sexy fuchsia lace negligee, her face perfectly made up.

'Victor, *querido*.' She extended a long, exquisitely manicured hand towards him. 'I've been so ill. Simply dreadful.'

'You don't look ill in the least,' he said dismissively, still not moving into the room.

'That's because I'm better now.' She made a moue with her mouth. 'Why are you standing there? Come on in and sit down on the bed. I want to talk to you.' She patted the covers invitingly.

'Isabella, you and I have nothing left to say to each other. I know very well that this accident was a story you and your sister made up to get me to come back here. You've made a big mistake.'

'But, Victor, darling, I had to see you to tell you that I've changed my mind. I thought I didn't love you any more, but—'

'Really?' His mouth took on a cynical twist and he threw his jacket down on the chair and closed the door sharply. 'Perhaps you should have thought of that before you killed my child.'

'Oh, but that's all in the past.' She waved her tapered fingers dismissively. 'I've decided that I don't want a divorce, that I love you after all. We can have another baby.' She flapped her long dark lashes in his direction, her beautiful eyes swimming with unshed tears.

She was good; Victor had to give it to her. But she'd have to find another fool to seduce with her wiles and tricks. 'Isabella, you're wasting your time. What happened to the boyfriend, by the way?'

'What boyfriend?' she responded innocently. 'You just made all that up to—'

'Shut up,' he hissed, coming into the middle of the room and staring down coldly at her. 'How dare you take me for a fool? Wasn't it enough that you aborted my child and went off with another man? Do you really think that for one minute I would consider taking you back? It's over, Isabella. Find someone else to provide you with all this.' He waved around the room at the vases of cut flowers and palms. 'I'm not impressed by your antics. Not one little bit. The show is over, and unless you get out of that damn bed and over to my lawyer's office first thing tomorrow morning, I'll refuse to pay the alimony I agreed upon.'

'You wouldn't.' She looked at him in astonished anger.

'Don't push me,' he muttered through clenched teeth. 'Just be glad that I happen to have other business to deal with in Rio, apart from your lies. I would recommend you be at my lawyer's office at nine o'clock tomorrow morning. I'll be there, and I plan to bring this whole business to a very fast close. It's over, Isabella. We're through.'

Then, picking up his jacket, he marched into the corridor, slamming the door hard behind him.

CHAPTER EIGHT

ARAMINTA soon discovered that becoming famous overnight had its pros and cons. On the one hand she was welcomed everywhere; her publishers had offered a huge advance for her following book and life was looking rosy. On the flipside she had little or no privacy—couldn't even ride on the Downs without some photographer popping out of the undergrowth to snap her picture.

Finally, realising that she could stand it no longer and would never get her next book written unless she took serious measures, Araminta decided to accept the offer of her friends, Ana and Tim Strathmuir, to stay in a cottage on their Scottish estate and disappear for a while.

There had been no sign of Victor, not a word since he had disappeared from her life so abruptly. And that was almost a month ago. Not that she spent her days thinking about him, but much against her will she found herself dreaming of him at night, recalling those exquisite moments shared in the turret room, the feel of his hands caressing her body. She would wake up feeling soft and yielding, filled with desire for this man who had flitted so quickly through her life, and, she knew, would never appear there again.

Now, as she arrived at Strathmuir Castle, and her new Land Rover headed through the gates to the estate, she experienced a sense of relief at having flown the coop, at being here in the wilds of Scotland, completely on her own, without any press pestering her and without the possibility, however remote, of running into Victor at some unsuspecting moment in Sussex.

Her mother, having finally realised that Araminta had become a star, was now basking in the reflected glory of her daughter's fame. Araminta smiled to herself cynically. All at once she'd become a paragon in Lady Drusilla's eyes, and could do no wrong. Thank goodness she'd decided to take the plunge and come up here by herself, even if it had meant facing driving on icy December roads.

Now, as she travelled slowly up the drive of the Scottish estate, she could tell that a snowstorm was brewing. Thank heavens she'd made it here just in time. The keys were at Home Farm with the factor, she'd been told.

Araminta peered through the looming mist at a building to her left. That must be it, she deduced, seeing a smoking chimney and lights in the windows even though it was only half past three in the afternoon. Turning up the bumpy lane, she parked in front of the door, then pulled on her thick anorak, jumped out of the Land Rover and stretched her legs, stiff from many hours of driving.

She stepped onto the front step and rang the bell. A dog barked from somewhere deep inside the house and she heard the sound of footsteps approaching. Soon the door opened and a cheery-faced woman with grey curls, a tweed skirt and thick Shetland jersey greeted her.

'Och, you must be Mrs Dampierre,' the woman exclaimed. 'I'm Rhona MacTavish. Now, come along in and dinna catch yer death out there, dearie.' She tutted, stepping aside for Araminta to enter.

'Thank you. That's most kind.' Indeed, the inside of the farmhouse was a sharp contrast to the dark, damp, misty weather outside. 'I believe you have the keys of Heather Cottage?' she said, smiling.

'Indeed I do, dearie. Now, you sit yersel' doon by the fire while I fetch them. And what about a cup of tea and a wee dram to keep out the cold?' Mrs MacTavish added with a broad smile.

'That would be lovely,' Araminta agreed gratefully.

'Then I'll put on the kettle while ye warm up.' She bustled off into the kitchen while Araminta rubbed her cold hands by the fire and looked about her at the walls, covered in pictures of men in kilts playing bagpipes, certificates and prizes won at the Highland Games, and a few paintings of scenes on Scottish moors dotted with shaggy Highland cattle.

With a sigh Araminta let go some of the tension that had weighed on her for the past few weeks. It felt wonderful to be miles away from the hype, in such a simple warm environment, where no one knew who she was. Mrs MacTavish, bless her heart, hadn't even recognised her or asked for an autograph.

With a contented smile she leaned back against the overbright plush orange velvet sofa and gazed into the low-burning coal fire. A few weeks spent here in Scotland would afford her a measure of peace, and the tranquillity she desperately needed to work on her next book, and would leave her no room for any thoughts of Victor. In fact the sooner she got cracking on it the better. Knowing that she already had the book outlined in her mind was a relief. It would help her get through the Christmas season with no regrets. And would prevent her spending it wondering where and how Victor and his wife were celebrating the occasion.

'Here's the tea, and a wee dram.' Mrs MacTavish came scurrying back into the room with a large tray piled high with fruit cake and scones, cream and butter, tea and a glass of whisky.

'You shouldn't have gone to all this trouble,' Araminta exclaimed, touched by her hostess's generosity.

'Well, ye look as if ye need a wee something to fatten ye up,' Mrs MacTavish answered, her face breaking once more into a cheerful smile.

Araminta swallowed, for the older woman's words reminded her of what Victor had said about quality and quantity, and for a moment she experienced a twinge of longing. But she banished it immediately. It was ridiculous to be hankering after the impossible. And Victor was exactly that: imperious, spoiled and impossible. The sooner she accepted that, the sooner she could forget about him and get on with her life and her success.

After finishing the tea, sipping the whisky, and being given the low-down on all the relations in Mrs MacTavish's photographs, Araminta finally got up.

'You've been far too kind, Mrs MacTavish, and I mustn't impose on you any longer.'

'Och, dinna you worry. I like a bit of company now and then. I'll just pop ma coat on and I'll be up to the cottage with ye. Hamish was supposed to put the lights on fer ye earlier, but ye ken what men are like.' She rolled her eyes, and before Araminta could stop her put on a heavy coat.

'Very well, but I'll drive you back down again.'

'Och, no, I'm used to the wee walk. It's not far—just across the field over there. Ye willna be too lonely, will ye?' she asked curiously as they closed the door and headed for the car.

'Not at all. In fact quite the opposite, Mrs MacTavish. I've come here to find some peace and quiet and to write.'

'Aye, that's right. Her Ladyship said ye were a writer. That explains it. Ye artisty types like to be alone. Creativity, that's what it is,' she said with a knowing nod as she climbed into the Land Rover.

Minutes later they drew up in front of a delightful stone cottage, just visible through the veil of heavy mist. Araminta jumped out, excited, and Mrs MacTavish followed with the keys.

'Looks as if Hamish has been here after all,' she remarked with a sniff, noting the gleaming light hanging above the front porch.

And, sure enough, when they opened it up the cottage was bright and welcoming. A fire crackled merrily in the grate of the charming, beamed living room, and Araminta wandered around enchanted. The place was delightful, small and old with gnarled beams and crooked walls covered in pretty fabric. The cottage had been most tastefully refurbished by Ana and Tim, she reflected, smiling, knowing at once that she would feel at home here.

'It's perfectly gorgeous, Mrs MacTavish. Lady Strathmuir's done a wonderful job,' she said after touring the upstairs rooms, delighted with the four-poster in the master bedroom.

'Aye, that she has. It took her a while, though, what with one thing and another.'

'I know I'll be happy here,' Araminta murmured, as though she needed to reassure herself.

'Well, that's good,' Mrs MacTavish answered, satisfied. 'Now, I'll be on ma way, or Hamish'll be hankering after his supper.'

'Please, you must let me drive you home.' Araminta moved towards the door.

'Och, lassie, you settle in now and dinna worry about me. The walk'll give me an appetite fer ma supper.'

Realising there was little use arguing, since Mrs MacTavish was obviously determined she should stay, Araminta thanked her once more, accompanied her to the door and stood for a few minutes watching the older woman disappear into the thickening mist at a strapping pace. She lingered a moment, assimilating her surroundings and breathing in the raw, damp evening air, then closed the door and locked it carefully.

Turning, she leaned against it and looked about her once more. Finally she was on her own, in a place that, for the moment at least, she could call home. With no rules, no regulations, no harping sound of her mother's voice, no criticisms or rebukes, and no pestering journalists to fob off.

Letting out a tired but happy sigh, she moved into the cosy living room and flopped onto one of the wide, plump chintz sofas next to the fire, determined to be as contented as she'd convinced herself she should be. But as she dropped her head back against the cushions and stared into the flames it was impossible not to conjecture, not to speculate, not to wonder about Victor's whereabouts and what he was doing at this very moment.

It was the twenty-second of December by the time Victor finally walked into his apartment in Eaton Place, tired but satisfied with the result of his unexpected journey. He'd only been away a month, but somehow it felt a lot longer. At least he'd achieved his objective and, thanks to some serious manoeuvring on the legal front, had finally managed to get the divorce decree.

At last he was rid of Isabella.

Whatever she got up to now and in the future was no more his affair—just as he would no more be responsible for her actions or her conniving.

He looked about him and sighed. It was almost Christmas, a time of year he usually found depressing. Christmas was only good if you had kids, or still had a family alive to go to. But for a bachelor in a city it was a time of reckoning, a time to rehash all the mistakes he'd made over the past few years and brood over them.

With another sigh Victor sat down in the large living room. He glanced at the mail on the coffee table but there was nothing of importance. Then he caught sight of a magazine next to the letters, and his eyes narrowed as he peered at the front cover in amazement.

He hadn't been mistaken! It *was* Araminta—holding a copy of her book.

He stared at the magazine for a moment, then dropped it back on the table. She'd never been far from his mind these past weeks. He'd decided it was better not to call her, to let sleeping dogs lie, and had tried resolutely to banish her from his thoughts. He'd become determined not to give the episode any importance, but without success. So she'd become famous overnight, had she? Well, he was pleased for her, of course. Perhaps now, with all this going on in her life, she would have forgotten him. So much the better.

Or was it?

All at once Victor regretted that he hadn't phoned or kept in touch. The past weeks had been filled with tying up and making a clean break with the past, ridding himself of the obnoxious problem of Isabella and making sure that it was done right. That had required his complete attention. Now that was done and he was back, maybe things could be different. Perhaps he should phone Araminta after all and explain? When he came to think of it, he had left her in rather an abrupt manner.

Victor got up. To his surprise he realised that he didn't want to let another hour go by without hearing the sound of that soft, husky voice—a voice that, if truth be told, had haunted his every free moment.

Picking up the phone, he dialled the number of Taverstock Hall, surprised when there was no reply. He let it ring for a while. Surely Araminta would be down in Sussex with her mother for Christmas? After several more tries he gave up. Maybe she was here in London, he reasoned, wondering if he had the number of the flat she'd been staying at and realising that in his hurry to depart he hadn't asked her for it.

Damn. This wasn't very promising.

Then he remembered Pearce and new hope flashed. Flipping through his organizer, he called his friend's mobile.

'Hello?'

'Pearce?'

'Yes, who is it?'

'Victor.'

'Aha, the return of the wanderer,' Pearce exclaimed. 'Where do you hail from?'

'I'm just back in London. I went to Brazil for a month.'

'I know. I heard through the grapevine.'

'You mean Araminta told you?'

'Yep. That's right. Didn't sound too pleased either.'

'Was she mad at me?'

'Well, that depends how you interpret mad. Was she about to throw a fit because you'd gone to Brazil? No, I wouldn't say *that*, exactly. Should she have?' Pearce asked, suddenly interested.

'No, no, of course not. Don't be ridiculous.' Victor forced himself to sound uninterested and casual. 'I just happened to mention to her that I might be going to Brazil, that's all.'

'I see. That explains it. Staying in town for Christmas, are you?'

'I haven't really thought about it yet,' Victor remarked, and looked about the room, which was devoid of any festive decorations. 'What about you?'

'Oh, I'm off to Wiltshire, as usual.'

'I see. By the way, I tried to ring Araminta at Taverstock Hall but there was no reply.'

'Not surprising. She's not there, and Lady Drusilla was probably hobnobbing at some Christmas do with the natives. By the by, you may not be aware, but there's been quite a bit going on since you upped and left for the southern hemisphere, old chap.'

'Really? What?'

'Well, thanks to my great management of her career, Araminta has become an overnight sensation. Not a child in this country can think of anything except *Phoebe Milk*. Bestseller on the Christmas lists.'

'That explains why I saw her picture on the cover of a magazine,' Victor responded gloomily.

'Just one?' Pearce laughed. 'The woman's a sensation—the latest phenomenon. And that's just the beginning. Wait till the film rights are negotiated, and the—'

'Yes, yes, I'm sure. But where is she?' Victor interrupted impatiently.

'Away.'

'I gathered that,' he responded, trying not to lose his calm. 'Where?'

'I'm not allowed to disclose her whereabouts.'

'Not allowed to— Why, that's perfectly ridiculous, Pearce. This is me, not some stranger,' he said arrogantly. 'I need to speak to her urgently.'

'What about? I'm her agent. If it's important I can deal with it,' Pearce said cautiously. 'Not trying to get your hands on the South American rights to her novel or anything like that, are you?'

'For God's sake, man, it's none of your business what I want to talk to her about. Damn the rights,' Victor growled. 'Now, come on, Huntingdon, give me her number.'

'Sorry, no go, old chap. But if you give me yours I suppose I could pass it on to her. That way, if she really wants to get in touch she will,' Pearce said, tongue in cheek, knowing exactly how annoyed Victor would be at not getting his own way.

'Oh, very well,' Victor conceded grudgingly. It wasn't satisfactory, but it was better than nothing. All he could do was hope that she might decide to call. But, despite his usual self-confidence, he didn't have any great hopes.

CHAPTER NINE

'ARAMINTA, I spoke to Victor Santander. He wants to talk to you,' Pearce announced during a call the next morning.

Sitting up in bed, Araminta blinked. Her heart leaped and she swallowed. 'When did he phone?' she said stupidly, fingering the duvet.

'Last night. I didn't want to disturb you.'

'Oh.'

'You sound disappointed.'

'Of course I'm not disappointed,' she snapped, irritated. The mere mention of Victor's name was conjuring up images she'd rather forget.

'Well, as I mentioned, he phoned last night, said he was back in town and wanted your number since he couldn't locate you either at Taverstock Hall or on your mobile. Of course I wasn't about to give him the number of Heather Cottage.'

'Oh. No, of course not.'

'Should I have? You said not to give it to anyone.'

'Of course. You were quite right.'

'I had no idea if you wanted to speak to him or not.'

'I don't,' she lied, trying to convince herself that the words were indeed true.

'Well, anyway, I've got his number. I can give it to you if you want, and then you can call him or not—as you wish,' Pearce said, dying to know more.

'Okay,' she replied, trying to sound bored. 'Just let me grab a pen.' She made a fuss of picking up the pad and pen that she kept on her bedside table while trying to calm her racing pulse. 'All right, go ahead.'

Pearce gave her the number and she jotted it down. So he was in London. She was dying to ask Pearce if Victor had said what he was doing for Christmas, then in a rush she remembered. He'd probably brought his wife with him. They'd be spending Christmas together.

His wife.

But as she hung up she realised with a measure of relief that this didn't make sense. If his wife was in London, surely he wouldn't be calling and leaving his number for her?

Araminta sank back among the pillows and stayed staring at the figures in front of her. So he'd returned. He'd disappeared for a whole month, hadn't shown any sign of life, and now he expected her to phone him.

The man really had a nerve.

Placing the number on the bedside table, she climbed out of bed and stretched, before heading downstairs to make herself a cup of coffee. As she boiled the kettle, added milk and sugar and popped a slice of bread in the toaster Araminta mulled over the idea of phoning him, weighing up all the options.

One minute she thought she would. The next she decided that no way would she lower herself to telephoning him after the way he'd behaved. She should banish the whole idea completely since he was married; what was the use of calling a married man and getting involved in a situation she knew could only end in tears?

By the time she'd sat down at the kitchen table and spread a thin layer of butter and jam on her toast she'd come full circle and still could not decide what to do. Perhaps she'd go for a walk, in the hope that the raw, bracing Scottish air would help blow away the cobwebs and clear her brain.

An hour later she was tramping in her shooting boots across the moors, trying not to give in to weakness. She would not phone him—would not expose herself to Victor Santander who, as far as she was concerned, could stew in his own juice. Talking to him would only revive those tumultuous feelings she'd tried so hard and so diligently to suppress.

In other words it was counter-productive.

Pleased with herself, and her strength of mind, Araminta took a deep breath of fresh air and headed purposefully back towards Heather Cottage, determined to get on with what she'd come here for in the first place: her writing.

From now on she would simply forget that the man existed and dedicate herself to writing only.

Having worked laboriously nearly all day on the synopsis of her new book, Araminta got up from her laptop tired but satisfied with the first results. Keeping busy was helping her forget that in two days it would be Christmas and she would be almost entirely alone.

Her eye wandered once more to the notepad with Victor's number, which sat glaring on her desk top. She had risen several times from her work, arguing that it might be better just to call him and get it over with, only to hang up before punching in the last digit, knowing she had no business encouraging him. He was married, and he'd hurt her enough already with his callous attitude and abrupt departure.

'Blast it,' she muttered, turning her back on the number, which by now she knew by heart. She sighed. What she could use right now was a drink and some supper. Stretching her stiff limbs, Araminta headed towards the kitchen, All at once the doorbell rang.

Surprised, she stopped in the hall and glanced at her watch. It was almost eight o'clock. Not a time when anybody would normally drop by. Plus, she didn't know anyone who'd call unannounced. Then she remembered. It must be Hamish, with the mince pies Mrs MacTavish had so kindly promised.

Heading to the front door she opened it with a smile.

'Do you always open your door to strangers so easily?'

Araminta quite literally froze at the sight of Victor Santander, leaning casually against the doorjamb and smiling a wickedly seductive smile that left her pulse leaping and her limbs weak.

'Wh-what are you doing here?' she muttered, backing into the hall as if she'd been stung.

'Isn't that fairly obvious? I came to see you.'

'But how—'

'Aren't you going to ask me in, *querida*?' he continued, not giving her the chance to speak. 'It's rather chilly out here.'

'Who gave you my address and why did you come?' she spluttered, trying desperately to quiet her heart and her lurching stomach and make some sense of the situation.

'If you'll allow me in, I'll endeavour to answer all your questions,' he responded, his tanned features breaking into another smile and his dark eyes flashing gold as he looked her over appreciatively.

'Oh, for goodness' sake, come in,' she muttered crossly. 'And close the door, please. I've had enough surprises for one evening.'

Entering the flagstoned hall, Victor removed his Barbour jacket and hung it on the newel post. Underneath he wore a high-neck, heavy-knit off-white sweater that accentuated his tanned skin and glistening chestnut eyes. If anything he was more devastatingly good-looking than she'd remembered him, Araminta realised, with a hastily suppressed shiver of longing.

'Since you're here, you'd better come and have a drink,' she threw at him grudgingly.

'Thanks. I could do with one. It's very cold out there.' He rubbed his hands together.

'How did you get here?'

'I flew to Edinburgh in my plane and then hired a car.'

'I see,' she said, looking at him coldly. 'I suppose I have Pearce to thank for this.'

'Don't blame him. I didn't let him off the hook until he finally spilled the beans. He didn't give me the phone number, though. Said he'd promised he wouldn't.'

'I'm impressed. I must be sure to enquire from him exactly what part of my whereabouts Pearce feels he should or should not reveal,' she murmured sarcastically. 'I thought I'd made it plain that I came here to be by myself, to get my book written and have some peace and quiet.'

'I know you did.' Victor's voice softened as he joined her next to a silver tray where various decanters and crystal tumblers stood. 'But I didn't come here to disturb you. I—'

'No? Then why exactly did you come?' She whirled around and faced him, her colour heightened by surprise and anger, and the knowledge that her emotions were as out of control as ever they had been causing her eyes to flash.

'Merely to say sorry for the rude way I left you last time we met,' he replied quietly.

Her hand faltered as she poured whisky into a tumbler. 'How very gracious of you. You could have done it just as well by phone.'

'Hardly, since I didn't have your number.'

'You could have waited until I phoned you,' she reasoned, wishing he wouldn't stand so close, that the scent of his aftershave didn't conjure up delicious erotic memories, that the mere sight of him wouldn't leave her weak at the knees.

'Would you have phoned me?' he challenged, raising a thick black brow, his flashing eyes boring into hers and his hand dropping onto her shoulder.

'I have no idea,' she replied crossly, annoyed at being caught in a trap of her own making, and a shiver running down her spine at his touch. 'It's of no consequence, since we have nothing to say to one another anyway.'

'Don't you think you're being a little hasty?' he queried, in a low, tantalising voice. He gave her shoulder a brief caress that sent heat soaring through her, as though determined to remind her of just how exciting his touch could be. Then taking the whisky from her limp grasp, he nursed it carefully, eyeing her while he assessed the situation. 'After all, we—'

'After all, nothing,' she interrupted angrily, moving next to the fire to create as much distance between them as the small room allowed. 'You are a married man, Victor Santander. You have commitments and obligations. It is none of my business how you run your life, but I can assure you I have no intention of being any part of it.'

'I see.' Victor said slowly, sending her a speculative look. So she thought he was still married. He was about to correct this delusion, when all at once he decided against it. Better to let things mature somewhat. This wasn't the moment for confessions.

'Look, I'm sorry if I've insulted you in some way,' he continued smoothly. 'I didn't come here to quarrel. Can't we call a truce? After all, it's Christmas,' he said, with a rueful smile that crinkled the corners of his eyes. 'Even enemies call a truce at Christmas.'

She looked at him a moment, and despite every instinct shouting at her not to listen to him her heart softened. 'What had you in mind?' she asked, suddenly thinking how nice it would be not to be by herself at Christmas after all.

'Well,' he said slowly, 'I'm alone for Christmas, and apparently so are you.' He raised a questioning brow. 'I thought perhaps we might join forces and share the holiday together, *querida*.'

'Did you, now? And where were you planning on staying?' she asked sweetly, still taken aback by his sheer nerve, but unable to suppress her sense of humour.

'I *could* go to a local hotel,' he said, with a smile and a look that would have melted the hardest woman's heart.

Araminta thought for a few seconds, then, despite her reluctance, gave in. 'You might as well stay here,' she muttered grudgingly. 'The only hotel is ten miles away, and there are two bedrooms in this cottage after all.'

'Good. Then I'll bring my stuff in from the car,' he said matter-of-factly.

'Now, wait a minute—'

'Yes? You did just invite me to stay didn't you?'

'Oh... Yes, I did.' Araminta threw up her arms in despair, too confused to understand her own actions.

'*Querida*, don't get upset,' Victor purred, moving closer and putting his hands on her upper arms. 'Nothing is going to happen that you don't want to happen. I promise.'

'I'm very well aware of that,' she bit back, pulling away, omitting to add what was uppermost in her mind. She could hardly tell him that it wasn't him she was worried about but herself, could she?

Just seeing him here in the cottage, feeling his presence in the same room, was enough to send off a myriad of inner signals that she'd much rather had stayed safely locked away. Oh, well. It was too late now to renege, so she'd better make the best of it.

'So, what's on the menu for Christmas lunch?' Victor asked, once he'd brought in his stuff and they were comfortably settled in front of the fire.

'I haven't a clue. I wasn't planning on having one.'

'Not planning Christmas lunch?' he said with mock severity. 'Oh, but I insist.' He looked across at her, eyes sparkling with a mixture of amusement and something more. 'I tell you what, we'll go to Edinburgh tomorrow and do some Christmas shopping.'

'I can't see the point of it.' Araminta replied huffily, still doggedly trying to fight Victor's contagious enthusiasm, trying not to recognise that his commanding presence had filled the small cottage with a new, warm and empowering energy that she was finding very hard to resist.

'Come on, Araminta, give me a break,' Victor replied, taking a long sip of whisky and watching her carefully over the rim of the crystal tumbler. He reached out his hand and touched her knee, sending shudders through her. 'Let's have fun—enjoy this time together.'

'Look, I don't want to start that *let's live the moment* thing again, okay? It may work for you, but it doesn't for me.'

'You mean you need all sorts of justifications?'

'I never said that.' She pulled her knee out of reach and turned towards the fire.

'Then what do you suggest? That we spend the holiday with you telling me all about your failed marriage and me recounting mine?'

'I never said that. And who says my marriage was a failure?' She slammed down her glass on the coffee table and let out a huff.

'Well, that's exactly what it sounded like. Any other suggestions?'

'No, I haven't. I think you're perfectly odious, and I wish I hadn't said you could stay,' she threw crossly, eyes filling all at once with unshed tears.

Victor watched her, concerned. Maybe he'd been too brusque, too brash. He felt suddenly annoyed with himself, wondering why he'd pushed her. What was it about this woman that made him react so unusually? Was he taking his anger at Isabella out on Araminta?

Rising, he moved to where she'd taken refuge by the fire. 'I'm sorry, *minha linda*. I didn't mean to hurt your feelings, *querida*.' He slipped his arm around her shoulders and drew her close. 'I suppose I've become a bit too pragmatic over the years.' He reached out and his finger etched her cheek, a strange sensation akin to nothing he'd felt in many years holding him in its grip. Then, realising that she was about to shy away once more, he placed his arms firmly around her and drew her close. 'Don't send me away, Araminta. I behaved badly with you before and I'm sorry. Please, give me another chance.'

'Why?' she responded, jerking her head up. 'Why, when all you want is pleasure in the moment? You said so.'

He drew in a sharp breath and stared down at her. 'I'm not sure that I'm ready for anything more than sharing a moment, *querida*. It wouldn't be fair to you if I pretended otherwise. But can't we enjoy whatever time we've got?' He drew back, looked deep into her eyes, seeking her response.

'Well?' He smiled at her now, a very different smile, a commanding yet tender smile that demanded an answer. And before she could resist he drew her head gently onto his shoulder and cradled it there.

'For whatever reason, Araminta, we need each other right now,' he murmured softly into her golden mane. 'Please don't fight it, *querida*. Rather accept it. And let the future take care of itself.'

At first she stood stiffly in his arms. Then slowly, knowing she wanted this more than anything in the world, knowing she could not resist the warmth and the scent of him, the aura of his presence, she allowed herself to relax in his embrace. This was crazy, absolutely mad. Surely she had more personality, more spirit, than to let herself be persuaded into another whirlwind encounter that would very likely end in the same abrupt manner as the last, however sorry he pretended to be?

Then, aware that she couldn't fight it, she let out a long sigh. This time she would have no excuse to fall back on. She knew exactly where she was treading. But, whatever the result, at least this time she would be prepared.

And he was right.

They could enjoy their time together without necessarily letting matters go any further. For that, she knew, would be entirely up to her. And *that*, she reflected with a sinking heart, feeling the hard wall of his chest rubbing against her, far too close for comfort, was exactly where the danger lay.

That night Araminta bade Victor a cheerful, friendly goodnight and closed the master bedroom door firmly behind her. She was not allowing herself any opportunities to give way to temptation. As an afterthought she even turned the key in the lock, remembering the morning at Le Moulin, determined not to let herself in for a repetition of that.

But no nocturnal visits disturbed her rest. Silence reigned and soon she fell asleep, content in the knowledge that he was next door, even if it left her wishing he was filling the bed beside her.

Victor did not get to sleep quite so easily. Having picked up a copy of *Phoebe Milk and the Magician's Promise* from her table, he read for a while, delighted by how magical the book was but unable to fully concentrate. For a moment he thought of getting up and knocking on her door, but knew he would be jumping the gun. She was still reticent, still afraid of being hurt.

And she was right to be.

He'd hurt many women over the past couple of years, had let the anger of his failed marriage out on others instead of channelling it into other directions. And he had no intention of doing it again. Tomorrow he would explain the situation to her and take it from there.

Still, the thought of her lying curled up in the big four-poster, wearing that deliciously virginal flannel nightdress he'd seen her in earlier, made him long to remove it and rediscover the delights of what he knew lay below.

Next morning was Christmas Eve and, despite trying to minimise its importance, Araminta, who loved the enchantment of the holiday and was dreaming up a delightful Christmas scene for her new volume, tripped downstairs in a much happier mood—which she tried not to attribute to Victor's presence. She was actually quite proud of herself. After all, she had not given in to any longings, and was fast coming to believe that she had the whole situation under control. Which was great, since it would allow her to enjoy the next few days with Victor with no regrets.

She found him in the kitchen, preparing breakfast.

'Good morning, *querida.*' He grinned at her from the stove. 'Do you like your eggs fried or scrambled?'

'Uh, scrambled, please,' she answered, utterly surprised to see the pine table attractively laid with a pretty Provençal tablecloth, mugs, plates and cutlery all set in place, and smell the delicious aroma of toast, eggs and fresh coffee—which she immediately recognised as Santander Gold—brewing.

'Sit down, and don't lift a finger,' he ordered authoritatively, dark brows reaching across the bridge of his nose as he concentrated on stirring the eggs. 'This will be ready in just a minute. The best eggs you've ever had,' he added modestly.

'Humble, as usual,' she commented, following his instruction and sitting down, unable to contain the gurgle of laughter that the sight of him expertly wielding a wooden spoon was causing.

'Now, don't distract me, *linda*,' he muttered, frowning, 'this is the *moment critique*. Ah! Perfect. *Voila!*' He swooped the eggs out of the pan, onto the plate and placed them before her. 'What else can I get for you, *madame*? Some salmon? A little caviar to add to these?'

'Sit down, or your eggs will get cold.' She giggled, watching his comical stance as he stood there in a silk dressing gown, still holding the wooden spoon at an angle.

'Very well, *querida*. Your wishes are my commands.'

'Well, in that case my wish is that you sit down and eat your eggs, and that later we do what you said and go into Edinburgh. If we're going to do this thing right we'd better get on with it. And soon,' she added, glancing at her watch, 'or all the shops will close.'

'That's the spirit, *querida*. And the first thing we need is a Christmas tree.'

'But we'll never find a Christmas tree now. It's too late,' she exclaimed between mouthfuls.

'Of course it's not.' Victor waved a dismissive hand. 'I'll ring Harrods and tell them to deliver one immediately.'

'Victor, that's absurd. How can Harrods possibly deliver a Christmas tree here at such short notice?'

'I see no reason why not,' he remarked with arrogant surprise. 'After all, I'm a very good customer.'

'I'm sure,' she muttered dryly. 'But why don't we go a simpler route and ask Mrs MacTavish if there is one to be had either on the estate or perhaps in the village?'

He looked at her, impressed. 'Good thinking. I see that fame hasn't yet corrupted you. You're still of a practical mind-set.'

'Fame?' For a minute Araminta had forgotten all about *Phoebe Milk* and the amazing success she was experiencing.

'Don't pretend. I know all about the book. In fact I read part of it last night and it's damn good. You deserve all the kudos—despite Pearce's conviction that he's entirely responsible for your career taking off.' He laughed.

'Well, I suppose in part he is. I never would have known how to go about it.'

'Congratulations.' He lifted his coffee cup. 'I should have said something sooner.'

'Oh, forget all that,' she dismissed. 'I'm glad to be away from the hype. At least the MacTavishes don't know about the book, which is a relief.'

'I wouldn't count on it. Their grandchildren are coming for Christmas. Wait till they hear that the author of *Phoebe Milk* is right on their doorstep,' he teased.

'How do you know about Mrs Mac T's grandchildren?' she asked, putting down her toast, surprised.

'I stopped by there on my way here. Otherwise I wouldn't have known how to get to the cottage.' He grinned and wiggled his eyebrows, enjoying her reaction.

'You mean you wheedled your way into her good graces, I'll bet. You don't miss a beat, do you?' she remarked tartly. 'Now, let's get this washed up and get going—or we won't find a piece of tinsel left in the shops, let alone a Christmas pudding. I dread to think what Princes Street must be like today.'

Later, as they sat in the Café Royal enjoying a late lunch, surrounded by packages filled with Christmas decorations and a number of gifts—Victor had insisted they split up for an hour to buy the other a surprise present—and mellowed by a bottle of Château Lafitte, Araminta recognised that she was awfully glad Victor had stayed, even if it was only a temporary state of affairs. She also recognised all the reasons why she should have sent him packing, but decided to ignore them for now and simply enjoy feeling warmed by his presence.

After coffee they decided it was time to return to Heather Cottage, before the traffic got too bad.

Araminta looked through the window and grimaced. 'Better be on our way,' she remarked. For outside the weather loomed grey and dreary, evening was fast closing in and sleet was beginning to fall. But as they were paying the bill and preparing to leave, three little girls in brightly coloured anoraks sidled shyly up to the table.

'Excuse me,' the tallest one with carrot pig-tails asked, 'are you Araminta Hamlin?'

'Yes. I am.' Araminta wrote under her grandmother's name of Hamlin.

'Please will you sign my copy of *Phoebe Milk*?' the little girl asked hopefully extending the book towards her.

'Of course. What's your name?'

'Lizzy.'

With a smile and a suppressed sigh Araminta signed the book and watched the three children scuttle proudly back to their parents' sides. 'I suppose I'd better get used to it,' she remarked to Victor. 'But it's all happened so fast that I can't quite believe it's true.'

'You will.'

'I guess.' She saw the occupants of another table eyeing her and hastily got up. 'Let's go, before somebody has the bright idea of phoning the press. Then we'll have no peace whatsoever.'

'You're right.' Taking quick stock of the situation, Victor rose and, picking up their several packages, they left the restaurant.

Victor watched her, amused at how anxious Araminta was to escape. He found it intriguing that she should spurn the fame and kudos that so many in her position would have welcomed. For a moment Isabella flashed to mind. If she'd had a third of Araminta's success she would have been crowing from the rooftops of Ipanema and finding every opportunity to get herself noticed...

Back at Heather Cottage they were thrilled to see that Mr MacTavish had left a lovely Scotch Pine tree on the doorstep.

'It's perfect,' Araminta exclaimed, now thoroughly caught up in the Christmas spirit. 'Let's trim it immediately.'

Together they mounted the tree in a corner of the living room, and Araminta climbed up a small stepladder while Victor passed her the trimmings that she'd so carefully selected from the Christmas display in Jenner's department store.

Looking up at her, he experienced a sudden tug of desire. It wasn't going to be easy to stay close to her and not touch, he reflected, smothering a sigh and swallowing as she stretched to a far-reaching branch, revealing a delicious strip of midriff.

Had he only known it, he was not alone in experiencing that desire. Every time their fingers met Araminta had to suppress the thrill searing through her. But she dismissed it summarily, attempting desperately to ignore the sensation, persuading herself that things were just fine like this: amicable, friendly, and not too personal.

She had just placed the angel on the top of the tree, and convinced herself that no intimacy was much the best way to go, when she lost her balance on the stepladder.

'Oh!' she squealed, tottering and falling straight into Victor's strong arms, her top riding up.

He held her there, gazing into her deep blue translucent eyes, reading all the doubts and fears. 'Just let it happen,' he whispered. Then, before she could react, before she could do more than stare into those devastatingly handsome dark features and flashing golden-flecked eyes, he brought his lips down on hers and, holding her tight, lowered them both onto the sofa and concentrated on the kiss.

Araminta lay tense in his arms, willing herself to break free. No, no, no. This couldn't be happening. Surely she had more will-power than this?

But as the kiss deepened, as his purposeful tongue explored the moist contours of her mouth, she recalled Le Moulin, and the delicious moments spent in his arms, the indescribable pleasure she'd experienced. A flaring arrow of white heat speared through her pelvis, leaving her shamefully wet and wanting, able only to cleave to him, her nipples strained taut against the hard wall of his chest, her senses delighted into silent expectant submission.

But Victor was in no hurry to move. For he too was remembering, recalling all too well the time she'd spent in his arms. Before that moment warmth had been lacking for so long in his life, then all at once it had surged out of nowhere when he'd least expected it. Slowly, lazily, he fought down any last barriers of resistance, a flash of male satisfaction transfixing him when he heard her sigh of surrender.

His hands roamed below the surface of her soft pink cashmere jersey, unhooked the front of her bra, leaving her distended breasts free to enjoy the full extent of his caresses. He brushed his fingertips lightly over the swollen peaks, sending shockwaves right down to her core. Araminta gasped, then arched as he raised her sweater and his gaze fell upon her swollen breast.

'Beautiful—you are simply beautiful, *querida*,' he whispered hoarsely, before lowering his lips and suckling the tip of each breast, tongue gently teasing, teeth taunting, until a tiny whimper escaped her and the coiling darts of desire spiralling between her thighs suddenly gave way.

Then Victor was tearing their clothes off, dropping them in a careless pile before the fire, his fingers seeking, caressing, delighting in the molten damp heat that welcomed him.

Araminta wanted him—wanted him more than she could describe. But how could she feel this way for a man who was tied to another woman, a man she didn't...love?

The word flashed as he entered her, hard and fast, and she knew that last was not entirely true. Bringing her legs up around him, she suddenly realised that her feelings for this man were far stronger than anything she'd cared to admit. But even as he penetrated deep within her, even as she felt that delicious build-up, that rush, followed by an explosion so violent as to leave her limp, she knew that she must not allow her growing feelings to show.

For even if for her this meant much more than just a pastime, for him it was nothing but that: a way of not spending Christmas alone.

As she came back to earth after the shattering experience Araminta forced herself to look the truth in the face. Once Christmas and their interlude were over then she must bring this adventure—she could hardly call it a relationship—to a complete end, or she'd get burned.

Badly burned.

'Araminta, *linda*—that is such a lovely, unusual name,' Victor whispered, his voice husky, relaxing in the aftermath of their lovemaking, playing with the golden strands of her hair shimmering in the firelight.

Logs crackled, the decorations on the tree sparkled and the CD they'd bought—a collection of classical Christmas melodies—was playing softly in the background. Suddenly he wondered at himself: what was he doing here? Why exactly had he come?

He wanted to reassure himself, to be convinced it had been just a spur-of-the-moment thing, a decision not taken upon sober reflection but out of a desire to be with someone—anyone—during a season that for some reason always left him sad. Yet was it only that? As he pulled a soft fur throw over them and brought his arms about her delicious pliable body, Victor reminded himself severely that that was all it could be.

He knew the score. And just because it was Christmas that didn't mean he should become sentimental. He'd been determined to stay shielded in a world where no feelings or emotions could reach him, but something about Araminta had snuck past his guard. However, he knew very well what women were like, how at first they appeared to be one thing then turned out to be another. He had suffered too often and too long from Isabella's hypocritical behaviour, and that of others, to allow himself to be deceived ever again by emotional tugs that ended up dangling a very high price tag.

Letting out a long wistful sigh, he suddenly wished it were otherwise.

But it wasn't, and experience told him it never would be. As soon as Christmas was over he would leave, before this entanglement became another mess, another embarrassment in his already complicated life. He'd vowed that Isabella would be the last woman to corner him, hadn't he? And he planned to keep it that way.

That night they slept together, in the large four-poster of the master bedroom, cuddling close under the goosedown duvet.

It seemed so natural to feel his body contouring hers, his arms encircling her, moulding her, Araminta reflected with a little sigh of longing. Dangerously natural, she realised as sleep descended at last and she closed her eyes. So what if it was only a passing fling? At least she felt happier than she had in a long while. Happier, she realised unexpectedly, than she could remember.

Feeling her body pressed to his, Victor experienced another rush of warmth and pulled her closer into his arms, nuzzling the back of her neck.

'Goodnight,' he whispered, ignoring the tug of desire that the feel of her delicious bottom curved into him provoked. That, he reflected sleepily, would have to wait until tomorrow.

CHAPTER TEN

THEY spent Christmas Day as planned, cooking a turkey in the Aga oven, drinking chilled champagne, laughing at each other's jokes between kisses and cuddles.

It was the most delightful Christmas she'd ever spent, Araminta realised, as she stood before the stove and dipped a spoon into the gravy she'd prepared. So natural and cosy and fun. 'Hmm. I think that's about right.'

'Is it, *querida*? Let me try.' Victor sidled up behind her and slipped his arms around her waist.

'You don't trust my cooking?' she queried, handing him the spoon and thinking how wonderful and intimate it felt to be here in this cottage, away from the world, living a romantic idyll.

Even if that was all it was, it was worth every minute, she concluded, eyes sparkling with laughter as he tasted the gravy and nodded approvingly.

'Just a pinch more salt and it'll be perfect,' he teased, dropping a kiss on her head then turning to top up their champagne glasses. 'By the way, aren't you going to wish your mother a happy Christmas?'

'I suppose I'd better,' Araminta answered reluctantly. Frankly, the thought of anything spoiling this perfect moment went against the grain, but she realised, it had to be done. 'What about you?' she asked in an off-hand voice that she hoped didn't expose her true feelings. 'Are you going to phone your—family?'

Her hesitation on the last word did not go unnoticed and Victor looked up. 'No. Not now.'

'Of course. I'd forgotten the time change,' Araminta replied quickly, chiding herself for having asked. It was none of her business after all.

Picking up her glass, she wandered into the living room and picked up the phone with a sigh. Better get on with it. She dialled Taverstock Hall and listened to the ring at the other end.

'Happy Christmas, Mother.'

'Well, at last,' Lady Drusilla's querulous voice replied. 'I expected your call earlier,

Araminta. I would have thought that even now you're famous you'd at least remember to call your poor mother on Christmas morning. I haven't been feeling too well.'

'Mother, it's only twelve o'clock. I didn't phone earlier because I knew you'd be at church, attending the morning service.'

'If you remembered at all,' Lady Drusilla countered unreasonably.

Victor stood in the doorway, glass in hand, watching Araminta perched tense and stiff on the arm of the sofa. Lady Drusilla seemed to make her life hell, as far as he could gather. A rush of hot, unexpected resentment surfaced against the older woman for causing Araminta pain on Christmas Day, when she'd been so joyful and carefree only moments earlier. What right had the old witch to make her daughter feel guilty just when she was experiencing so much success and happiness?

Araminta put down the receiver and let out a sigh.

'Everything okay?' he asked, entering the room, his eyes never leaving her pale face, his resentment gathering.

'Fine.' Araminta gave a despondent little shrug. 'My mother never seems to be satisfied with me, whatever I do. Well, no point in dwelling on it, is there?' she said a little too brightly, and got up.

'I think maybe there is,' Victor answered carefully, handing her the champagne, then standing over her and studying her closely. 'No one should be allowed to get to you as your mother seems to.'

'I know. You're right,' she agreed, sinking among the cushions of the sofa and staring into the fire before taking a long sip of champagne.

'Then why do you let her?'

'I don't know.' She shrugged. 'Habit, I suppose. Guilt and all that.'

'Guilt for what?'

'Oh, I don't know. For not being the perfect daughter I suppose. I tried for ages, but I never seemed to get the drift of it. I thought after I married Peter that maybe—' She suddenly realised what tricky territory she was stepping into and closed her mouth.

'What did you think after marrying Peter?' he asked softly.

Araminta hesitated. She had not intended to talk about the past, or her marriage. 'Nothing, really.'

'That seems unlikely,' he answered dryly.

'Okay, then,' she said, flinging her glass down on the coffee table, suddenly cross at his insistence. 'I married Peter in part because Mother thought he was the ideal husband—the perfect English gentleman and all that.'

'And was he?'

'On the surface, I suppose. Look, I don't really know, okay?' She got up quickly, colour slashing her high cheekbones. 'It really doesn't matter any more, since the man's dead anyway.'

'And are you guilty of that too?' he asked, quirking a thick black brow.

'What on earth do you mean?' she asked, spinning around and facing him full-on.

'Just that. Do you feel in some way responsible for his death?'

'No. Of course I don't. Why should I? I had nothing to do with it. It wasn't my fault that his brakes failed. I didn't order there to be ice that night. I didn't have the lorry skid across the road,' she hurled, eyes bright with unshed tears.

'No, but you feel as if you did,' Victor said quietly, standing up and gripping her stiff shoulders. 'Araminta, you're caught in a web of guilt that dominates your whole existence.'

'Really? Do you know me so well that you can stand there doling out advice like a psychologist? You know nothing about me or my life,' she flung angrily. 'Why don't you just leave me alone? I don't even understand why you turned up here out of the blue anyway. I suppose you had nothing better to do for Christmas?'

'That's ridiculous,' he returned fiercely, dropping his hands, offended.

'Oh, really? Then why exactly did you come?' she threw, her flashing blue eyes blazing like two molten pools of fire. 'You don't seem very clear about your own motives for doing things, Victor Santander. Perhaps you should take a look in your own backyard before handing out gratuitous advice to others.'

Grabbing her glass, she flounced out of the room and returned to the kitchen. The man was presumptuous, full of himself and unbearable! The fact that he'd hit the nail on the head, touched a sore spot, made it far worse. It was true that she felt guilty for having quarrelled with Peter on the evening of his death, for perhaps having been the unwitting cause of his going out unnecessarily that night. But that didn't make her responsible.

Angrily, Araminta shoved some Brussels sprouts into a saucepan, which she plonked crossly onto the Aga with a thud. Damn Victor and his cheap psychology. She didn't need that. Least of all on Christmas Day, thank you very much. Instead of doling out high-handed opinions on matters he knew nothing about, he should be thinking of phoning his wife.

Araminta dug her nails into her palms and gritted her teeth. She damn well hoped he had a cellphone available, for she had no intention of letting him call on her landline.

For a moment she stared at the plum pudding, which had been steaming away for the past two and a half hours, and asked herself why she'd allowed him to stay. This was all her own fault, she realised with a ragged sigh, all her own doing. She should have told him to get lost the other night and then none of this would be happening. Had she but banished him on the spot she would not now be standing here making a ridiculous Christmas lunch that she didn't want to eat. Nor would she have spent time choosing a gift for him, a pale green cashmere sweater she'd thought he'd like. Or— Suddenly a rush of tears poured down her cheeks and her shoulders shook.

Victor stood near the sitting room fire, foot on the brass fender, and battled the unwelcome thoughts racing through his mind. She had every right to be angry, every right to be upset. And every right to ask the question of why he had come. The fact that he couldn't answer it himself didn't improve matters. Suddenly he didn't care what his reason for coming here was. He'd wanted to, and that was good enough.

With masterly steps he crossed the hall and entered the kitchen, only to see Araminta standing with her back turned and her shoulders shaking. A rush of compassion and anger at his own insensitive behaviour made him take a step forward.

'*Querida*, don't cry,' he said, standing close behind her, reaching his fingers into the mass of blonde hair falling about her shoulders.

'Don't.' She whirled round and pulled away. 'Don't touch me. I wish you'd just leave.'

'Araminta, *linda*, I'm not going anywhere.'

Before she could protest, Victor swept her into his arms and held her pressed to him, gazing down into her tormented face, her eyes so troubled and angered, such a total mass of confusion that all he could do was hold her close.

'You have no right,' she threw. 'No right to judge me.'

'I know,' he replied. Then before she could continue he planted a kiss firmly on her resistant lips, prying them open while his hands travelled up and down her spine, traced the curve of her bottom, pressed her hard against the firm muscles of his chest.

Araminta gasped, tried to pull back but to no avail. And just as her anger had soared so it diminished now, at the feel of his hands soothing her back in that possessive male manner that left her yearning for so much more, when she should actually have the stamina to reject him, send him away.

And mean it.

She could feel his hand travelling upwards underneath her top, knew that whatever she said, however much she remonstrated, the taut swell of her nipples told him better than words how she felt. When his thumb finally grazed the tightly swollen tip of her breast her head fell back and she let out a sigh of delight, unable to contain the ever-increasing spiral coiling within her. Why was it that all this man had to do was to touch her and she melted?

He was working on her other breast now, showing no mercy, titillating, taunting, until she throbbed low down between her thighs, felt herself go liquid and warm, could do no more than submit when he pulled up her kaftan and she felt his hard maleness seek her. As Victor pushed her against the fridge door Araminta gasped, a rush of delight overwhelming her as, in one swift thrust, he entered her and together they reached new heights. She clung, arms clenched around his neck, while he thrust deep within her, as though trying to expunge some memory, possess her in a way she'd never been taken before.

Then the spiral rose, and all at once she could bear it no longer. She dug her nails into his shoulders and came with an unrestrained cry of release. She could feel him joining her on this exquisite wave of emotion, rising with her on the crest. Together they crashed into the surf, gasping, dizzy with sheer, unadulterated satisfaction.

In the aftermath Araminta felt too weak to do more than lean against Victor's hard male body, her head drooping onto his muscled shoulder, listening to the beat of his heart match hers.

'That was incredible,' he whispered, lifting her in his arms and carrying her through to the living room, where he laid her down carefully on the sofa, kissing her all the while and drawing her head into his lap.

Araminta was too limp, too sated and deliciously saturated to do more than close her eyes and enjoy the incredible peace and fulfilment. How could she live without this now that she'd been given a taste of it? she asked herself suddenly.

Then all at once consciousness returned, and she sniffed warily.

'Oh, my God!' She sat up with a horrified start, realising that something was burning. 'The turkey!'

CHAPTER ELEVEN

'I HAVE to get back to London,' she told Victor the next day over breakfast. It was a decision taken on the spur of the moment. But once she'd decided Araminta knew she had to go through with it. Prolonging the interlude would only make it more difficult to depart if she became more involved with this man.

It was bad enough as it was.

Victor laid his cup carefully down in the saucer and, dark eyes piercing, looked straight at her. 'Why?' he asked peremptorily.

'Because I have some interviews to give for the book,' she lied glibly.

'On Boxing Day?' he enquired smoothly, raising a brow.

'No, not today. But in the next couple of days.'

'Ah! I see. So when you came up here it was only to spend a few days?' He nodded sagely, his eyes never leaving her face.

'Look, what I do is my own business, okay?'

Araminta's flustered behaviour only confirmed what he already sensed: that she was running away before she got in too deep. Well, maybe she was right, he reflected after an initial flash of pain. Methodically he spread some butter on a piece of wholewheat toast, forcing himself to think with his head and not his feelings, which seemed increasingly haywire. Maybe it was better this way. He certainly didn't want to have a serious affair with anyone...did he?

The sudden realisation that neither did he want the interlude to come to an end shocked him. Hadn't he sworn blind that he would never allow that to happen ever again? That no woman was worth the trouble?

Yet there was something about her, something that drew him in a way hitherto unknown, that was slowly eating at him.

'Okay,' he said suddenly, pushing the plate away and smiling blandly. 'When do you want to leave?'

Disguising her disappointment at his quick acquiescence to a plan she was fast beginning to regret, Araminta lifted her chin and pretended to be pleased.

'I think I'll probably set out this afternoon, if that's okay with you?' she asked sweetly, burying her pain and hurt pride behind a neutral smile.

He didn't care about her. That much was plain. The wonderful times spent in bed and out were just part of his ritual, the way he interacted with every woman. And she'd be a fool to take it for anything else.

'I think that might just be possible,' Victor concurred, in much the same half-serious, half-bantering tone that masked his urge to get up, whip her into his arms and forcefully make her forget any desire to go to London or anywhere else for that matter. 'Any specific time in mind?'

'Whatever suits you,' she responded, painfully polite. 'I think I'll pop upstairs, make a couple of calls and start getting my stuff ready.'

'I didn't realise that you needed a whole morning to pack,' he murmured, watching her rise, eyes following her slim, curvaceous figure as she walked to the dishwasher and placed her cup and plate in it. 'Tell me, how do you plan to live, now that you're famous and making tons of money?'

'In the same way I've always lived. Oh, you mean do I plan to find a place of my own?' she queried, turning round and leaning against the counter.

'Yes.'

'Well, of course I do.'

'In Sussex?' he asked casually.

'I—I don't really know yet. I might get a small pad in London and then see.'

The thought of buying a house anywhere in the vicinity of Victor was not in the realm of possibilities. Just looking at him, seeing him sitting so casually unaware of his effect on her, his devastating good looks and his lean muscular body, the jeans and grey T-shirt emphasising each well-etched muscle, left her swallowing and recalling each instance of their lovemaking over the past few days. She looked away. They were only a kitchen floor apart, but it felt like an ocean. All the intimacy of the past days had suddenly disappeared, and in its place loomed a vacant void.

With a tiny sigh Araminta put the milk in the fridge and wondered if her life was really going to change that much now that she was famous. Perhaps. Perhaps not. It all depended on so many outside factors over which she

didn't have full control. At least having a place
of her own would be a wonderful relief, and
would allow her time to write the several
books that were being proposed to her. Pearce
was even talking of a movie contract.

'You know, I don't think you've quite
grasped just what's happening to your life,'
Victor said, as though reading her mind. 'Like
it or not, your existence is taking a three-
hundred-and-sixty-degree spin. There will be
just so far you can run to escape.'

'Well, that'll be my problem, won't it?' she
said, flashing a brittle, bright smile.

'I guess. If that's how you want it to be.'

For a second she looked at him. What did
he mean by that? Probably nothing, she concluded, sweeping the crumbs from the table
and almost colliding with him as he rose to put
his cup and saucer in the dishwasher. Probably
nothing at all.

The emptiness she felt as she dragged up the
stairs left Araminta feeling sick and tired, as
though all the wondrous energy of the past
days had simply dwindled, like a spectre, into
the shadows. With a sigh she flopped onto her
bed in a lethargic heap, too enervated to fight
the black cloud of depression forming over

her. Why had she encountered a man who was a dangerous flirt and a playboy? Why couldn't she have come across somebody normal— somebody like Peter?

All at once she sat up, aware of what a coward she was. She had married Peter for all the wrong reasons: because he'd seemed safe, because her mother had approved, because— well, because it had been the easy way out. And what had been the result? A colourless relationship with little sexual satisfaction and her pretending to herself that everything was rosy so as not to upset the apple cart. Yet the apple cart had been upset despite all her attempts to maintain the status quo. Was that what she wanted? A repetition of the same? Surely she had more gumption than that?

But this man she had feelings for—knew that she would have a hard time living without—was not interested in anything but a casual affair consisting of occasional encounters here and there—a weekend in Normandy, a couple of stolen days in Paris or Rome. Was that what she wanted? Did she care for him sufficiently to accept the crumbs, knowing that she would never be offered the whole loaf? Because of course she would be expected to

disappear discreetly the minute his wife appeared, which at some point she was bound to
do.

Araminta dangled her feet glumly over the
edge of the bed. There was no way out, no
solution, and the sooner she recognised this
fact and faced it the sooner she'd get over this
man who was fast becoming an obsession.

Downstairs, Victor stirred the fire thoughtfully.
He still had several days before the New Year,
he justified, so he might as well make good
use of them. He wondered what Araminta was
doing upstairs. For a moment he almost broke
the resolution he'd made that morning not to
insist. Should he go up and see for himself
what she was up to? But he couldn't. Mustn't.
It wasn't fair on either of them. After all, he
had nothing to offer her.

Or did he?

Suddenly Victor stood up straighter, and for
the very first time registered that he actually
had a divorce decree. The damn thing had
come through, hadn't it. Was sitting safely
placed in the right-hand upper drawer of his
desk in Eaton Place. But that didn't mean he
had anything to offer, he reminded himself

quickly. He was finally free of the bonds which had tied him for too long. The last thing he planned was to enter into another relationship that would inevitably flounder.

With a sigh, his dark features set in rigid lines, he sat down in the nearest armchair. What was it about Araminta, about this whole time spent together, that had touched a part of him he'd been so sure was numbed for ever? Was it that sweet smile on those luscious lips? Or the haunting look that sometimes flitted through those huge deep blue eyes? Surely he was not dupe enough to fall for something as simple and superficial as that?

Yet, hard as he tried, he found it impossible to convince himself that her attributes were mere wiles. And the only thing that stopped him taking the stairs in several masterful strides, throwing her on the bed and making passionate love to her once again, was the knowledge that he'd be breaking the silent bargain struck between them.

They parted company several hours later, and many hours after that, having made the long journey back down from Scotland, Araminta stood alone in front of the building in Pont

Street where Sara's flat was situated, wondering what Victor was doing. It was an all-too-familiar feeling, Araminta reflected sadly as she let herself into the building.

And it would be this way for as long as she allowed it to continue.

Victor was not a man to be tied down. She almost felt sorry for his wife. What kind of a life must she have, with a man who was never there, never faithful, never a part of her own life?

As the elevator ascended Araminta convinced herself that she was very lucky not to be in that position herself. A man like Victor could only bring unhappiness into a woman's life.

As she entered the dark apartment she forced herself to remember the words they'd exchanged on parting.

'I'll call you later this evening,' Victor had pronounced abruptly. And she'd nodded, knowing perfectly well that he didn't mean it, that there was probably a pile of invitations waiting for him at Eaton Place.

Christmas might be a family time for most people, and inspire loneliness for some, but the end of the year was always awash with parties and activities. And an attractive single man was always a plus.

Switching on the light, she noticed the heap of mail on the dining room table that Sara had kindly stacked for her and, laying down her bags, she flipped through it. Her eyes narrowed as they fell on a handwritten envelope with a foreign stamp. The postmark was illegible so she turned it over.

Strange. No sender.

Curious, Araminta split the top of the envelope and pulled out a single sheet of white paper inside which were enclosed several photographs. Unfolding it, she caught a glimpse of the first snapshot and froze. It was of Victor, his arm loosely thrown over the shoulders of a very beautiful brunette with long glossy hair. They were gazing into each other's eyes.

Hands trembling, Araminta studied the other three pictures. More of the same—the woman with her arms linked about his neck and Victor smiling into her eyes, another of the pair embracing in what might have been a nightclub.

Feeling slightly faint, Araminta sat down with a thud on a dining room chair and, hand still shaking, read the sheet of paper. All it said was:

He is not what he seems. Be warned.

A friend

Whoever it was had not identified themselves.

Araminta experienced a moment's disgust at the low nature of the gesture. But as she glanced again at the pictures she realised she must be looking at Victor and his wife—that mysterious woman whose name she suddenly recalled was Isabella. Sudden rage gripped her. How could he be so callous? How could he simply play with women, tinker with their affections, then discard them like old shoes?

He was despicable.

Araminta took another long look at the pictures, determined to overcome the turmoil of pain and anger—and something else, something she'd never experienced before but that she suspected might very well be jealousy. How could she be jealous of a woman she didn't know? A woman who had every right to him? It was ridiculous.

Furious, she rose and marched into the kitchen, tore the pictures up deliberately into tiny shreds and threw them and the letter into the bin.

Good riddance. She had no need for any soap opera episodes in her life—anonymous letters from hurt wives or anything else. She was a woman in her own right, a writer who'd just become famous. What did she need this aggro for?

Then, still livid, she rushed to the bedroom and tore open her address book, damned if she would sit here waiting for a possible phone call that probably wouldn't come and that she didn't want even if it did. No. Although she hated the idea, she would call up friends and make sure she was invited out night after night. She'd even allow the press to photograph her, if that was what it took to keep Victor Santander at arm's length.

Picking up the phone, she punched in a number and waited as it rang, aware that from now on, as far as she was concerned, Victor Santander could rot in hell.

And enjoy it!

The phone rang and rang, but no one picked up.

It was three days since they'd left Scotland, and for three days he'd endeavoured to contact her—had tried everything from ringing her mobile to leaving notes in the letterbox at the flat. He'd even sent a telegram. But to no avail. Either Araminta had left London without a word, or she was simply refusing to take his calls.

But why? Why would she suddenly become incommunicado? Their parting had been somewhat formal, particularly when compared to the intimacy of their days spent together in the cosy warmth of Heather Cottage, but still nothing to merit complete silence.

Plus, to his discomfort, Victor didn't quite know how he felt any more. On the one hand he was annoyed with her, on the other strangely hurt. Not to mention his pride. That had taken a serious jolt. For, after all, no one in their right mind rejected Victor Santander out of hand. That simply didn't happen.

But he was unable to rally the energy to counter the onslaught of—surely it couldn't be depression? He'd never had anything like that! Unease, that was it—unease that Araminta was inconsiderately causing him. She was thoughtless, he argued, and selfishly thinking only of herself and her feelings. What about him? Didn't she realise that he'd become attached to her in the few times they'd shared a bed?

So attached, he realised, wary of his own admission, that he missed her dreadfully.

New Year's Eve came and went, with Victor in front of the fire at Eaton Place, nursing a very strong whisky and listening with a jaded ear to the merrymaking in the streets.

Where was she at this very moment? he wondered, gazing at his glass, furious that he was wallowing in discontent because of a woman. It had never happened before, and he vowed he would never let it happen again. Forget Araminta Dampierre. She was probably drunk on her new fame, enjoying being courted by every Tom, Dick and Harry, lapping up the glory of it all. She probably didn't remember he existed.

The thought made him so furious that he brought his fist down with a bang onto the mantelpiece where he'd been leaning thoughtfully. Damn Araminta, and damn his ex-wife. Damn women in general!

But even as he determined to change his lifestyle, to get out on the town and forget the whole affair, even as he marched to his room and undressed, the unwanted image of her stuck. Like Professor Higgins, he reflected bitterly, he'd grown accustomed to her face. And all he could think about as he tossed in bed that night was the way she'd gasped when he'd entered her, the way she moved, the warmth of her, and how he missed each curve of her sensual body moulded to his.

CHAPTER TWELVE

IT WAS fun, of course—had to be fun—being flown off to a Caribbean island for New Year's Eve in a private jet. But even as she threw herself into the spirit of things Araminta found it hard to derive any enjoyment from dancing on the beach till dawn, drinking exotic cocktails and sleeping until the early hours of the afternoon. In fact she was very glad when her return flight finally touched the tarmac in London and she could make a hasty retreat to the flat.

Ignoring the numerous, increasingly angry phone messages on the answering machine, and the notes in the letterbox, Araminta concentrated on planning the next few days. She knew it was time to go down to Sussex. She had to see her mother, even if it was only for a little while. Plus, she needed to organise her things. Once life picked up next week she'd start flat-hunting in London.

Pearce, who'd gone with her to Barbados, had asked her several pointed questions regarding Victor, but she'd answered them guardedly, careful not to show any emotion, warily hiding all the roiling feelings churning inside which wouldn't subside however hard she tried or however far she ran.

With a deep sigh Araminta flopped into an armchair and, after fiddling with Victor's written notes for several minutes, finally opened one.

It was as arrogant and demanding as she'd anticipated. So Victor Santander didn't like being the one rejected, did he? Well, serve him right. Give him a taste of his own medicine.

All at once Araminta leaned forward, suppressing the nausea which rose suddenly in her throat. It had happened several times now, leaving her in no doubt that too much alcohol and partying definitely didn't suit her. She could live without seeing another glass of champagne for a while.

She grimaced. Perhaps the best thing to do *was* to go down to Taverstock Hall right away and take a much-needed break. Not that being with Lady Drusilla would be much of a rest. But, still, she could ride and be quiet, and think about where her life was headed, without the fear of Victor haranguing her. For the last place he'd be at this time of year was at the Manor. Hadn't he mentioned he was off to Central America early in the New Year? Something to do with acquiring coffee for a special blend he was planning to launch on the market?

Later in the day, feeling considerably revived and determined not to think about him any more than she could help, Araminta relegated Victor's many missives to the rubbish bin and, locking up Sara's flat carefully behind her, left for Taverstock Hall.

'I thought perhaps you might have seen her over the past few days,' Victor said casually, eyeing Pearce carefully across the table, looking for any give-away signs the other man might unwittingly put out.

'I have, actually. We spent New Year's together.'

'You what?' Victor laid down his knife next to his lamb chop, eyes glittering.

'Mmm. It was quite a party, actually. We danced all night on some damn beach at Rollo Bolton's; you remember Rollo, don't you? He was in your house at school,' Pearce continued chattily, oblivious of the mounting anger opposite him.

'Do you mean to tell me that while I—?' Victor cut himself off and took a deep breath. 'Are you saying that you and Araminta are having an affair?' he asked, his voice dangerously quiet.

'What? An affair with Araminta?' Pearce looked up and burst out laughing. 'Good Lord, no, old chap. She just didn't want to stick around town for the festivities, so as I was going to Rollo's I asked if she could join us. Old chap was delighted—of course—thrilled to be able to rake in the latest celeb. Great hit, of course. Not that she seemed on cracking form, now I come to think of it—seemed a bit quiet. But that's writers for you. I *know*. I deal with them all the time.' Pearce rolled his eyes expressively. 'They're up one minute and down the next, like yoyos. How about ordering some trifle for pudding?' he added helpfully. 'Bingo Bingham told me it's jolly good here.'

Victor scorned the trifle with a dismissive wave. 'What I want to know, Pearce, is where Araminta can be found.'

'You seem awfully keen on her all of a sudden,' Pearce said thoughtfully, a canny look entering his amused grey eyes. 'Say, what's happened to the voluptuous Isabella? Sure you don't want to try this trifle? Don't mind if I have some, do you?'

'Damn the trifle. I want to know where I can find Araminta,' Victor insisted, leaning forward. 'And as for Isabella, she's history. I finally got a divorce.'

'Good Lord, you don't say?' Pearce held his trifle spoon in mid-air.

'It came through in December, when I was over in Brazil.'

Pearce let out a long, low whistle and laid down his spoon. 'Well. I must say, old chap, I never thought she'd let you off the hook.'

'I didn't give her a choice,' Victor muttered tightly. 'Now, will you please tell me where Araminta is? I've been trying to reach her for days, and all I get is her damned voicemail, both at that flat she was staying at and on her mobile. I even left notes in her letterbox,' he confessed, dragging his fingers through his hair.

'I see.' Pearce wiped his mouth on a large linen napkin. 'If I didn't know any better I'd say you'd fallen hard, old chap. Sorry I can't help you.'

'Pearce, you are not leaving this table until you tell me,' Victor said, his tone quiet and dangerous.

'Now, now, no South American antics, old boy. This is England, you know. Plus, I'm her agent. I can't go round telling everyone where she is. Wouldn't be right when she's asked me not to. Professional ethics and all that.'

'I am not everyone,' Victor retorted haughtily.

'No. But I'd be willing to bet that you're one of the reasons she's skipped town,' Pearce answered shrewdly, peering at Victor across the empty trifle dish, eyes narrowed.

It was now obvious to him why Araminta had seemed under the weather all the time they were away. He'd even wondered if she was sickening for something. Perhaps there was more going on than met the eye. He took another glance at Victor, staring thunderously at him across the table. Surely it couldn't do any harm if he gave the man a hint. He might even be doing them both a favour.

'Well?' Victor flexed his tense fingers and looked his friend in the eye.

'Let's just say,' Pearce murmured carefully, 'that she's visiting a close family member in the country. Now, don't ask me any more,' he said, raising his hands firmly, 'because you won't get another word out of me. Forget I said that, okay?'

'Thank you.' For the first time in his thirty-five-year existence, Victor felt true gratitude to another human being.

Araminta was shocked when she arrived at Taverstock Hall to find her mother in a much diminished state. She immediately felt an attack of guilt at having abandoned her during the holidays.

'Mother, I think you should see Dr Collins at once,' she said, looking worriedly at her mother, seated by the fire, her face hollow, her legs wrapped in a cashmere rug.

'I have, darling,' Lady Drusilla said weakly. She seemed so frail and different from the determined power-wielding woman Araminta was used to that she found it hard to equate the two.

'And what did he say?' she asked anxiously.

'I'm afraid it's not good news.'

'Wh-what?' Araminta sat on the edge of her chair her hands clasped tensely in her lap.

'I'm afraid I have cancer.'

'Oh, no.' Araminta rushed across the room and for the first time in memory clasped her mother's bony hands in hers. 'Is it—?' She left the end of the sentence unfinished, unable to say more.

'They don't really know. It's been bothering me for some time. I didn't want to tell you—spoil your success with the book. I know I've not always been very enthusiastic about your ventures, Araminta, but I'm so proud of you.' Lady Drusilla's eyes filled with tears and she squeezed her daughter's hand. 'It hasn't always been easy bringing you up on my own, you know. As a widow one has to be so careful, and I—' Her voice wobbled and Araminta closed her arms about her.

'Oh, Mother, I'm so sorry. Have you seen a specialist?'

'Yes. But I'm afraid he isn't very hopeful. I'm sorry to be such a nuisance to you.'

'Oh, Mother, how can you say that?' Araminta asked, distressed, horrified that for all these years they might have been close, yet a wall of misunderstanding had kept them apart.

*   *   *

Lady Drusilla Taverstock died in Araminta's arms two days later—on the morning that Victor Santander arrived at the Manor. Mother and daughter had exchanged so many confidences in those past few hours that Araminta could hardly believe life had given them this last, final opportunity to make up the rift of years. What if she hadn't decided to escape London and come home? What then?

She felt increasingly nauseous and ill, but knew it was nerves. She would be better once all this was over—once she'd had time to grieve for the woman she'd only recently learned to know before it was too late.

'*Senhor* Victor?' Manuel knocked on the door of the study and brought in a tray of coffee.

'Thank you, Manuel. Any news to report?' Victor glanced at his watch, wondering what time would be most suitable to catch Araminta at the Hall. He wanted to catch her unawares.

'Yes, *senhor*, actually there is. I just heard from the cleaner that Lady Drusilla, over at Taverstock Hall, died last night.'

'Lady Drusilla? Dead?' Victor exclaimed, horrified.

'Yes. Apparently she had cancer, but no one knew. Her daughter was with her at the end, though, which was a mercy, poor woman.' He crossed himself.

'Thank you, Manuel, that will be all,' Victor murmured, turning towards the window in shocked disbelief. He must get to her—go to her at once.

Without a second thought Victor rushed through the hall and, grabbing his shooting jacket, ran down the front steps and into the Range Rover.

Minutes later he was pulling up in front of the Hall, where several vehicles were parked. Perhaps this was not a good moment, but he really didn't care—just wanted to be near her, give her the solace she needed at this time.

Olive opened the door and showed him into the study. 'I'll just get Miss Araminta,' she murmured, her tear-stained cheeks telling him more than words how distressed the household was.

Olive left him in the study and crossed the hall to the drawing room, where Araminta was seated with the vicar, planning the funeral service.

'There's a gentleman for you in the study,' Olive murmured, before retreating, hanky in hand, towards the kitchen.

'If you'll excuse me a moment, Vicar?' Araminta said with a sigh. There was so much to cope with, so much to do, and so little time to grieve properly for the woman she'd just learned to know.

'Araminta, I think that about wraps up the arrangements for the funeral. Now, you get some rest and we'll go over this again tomorrow. Don't bother to show me out,' the vicar said kindly.

'Thanks. You've been wonderful.' She shook his hand gratefully.

Then she moved across the hall to the study, wondering if it was the man she was expecting from the undertaker's.

The sight of Victor standing in the middle of the room was so unexpected that she drew in her breath.

'Araminta, darling. I came as soon as I knew.'

Before she could breathe, before she could respond, Victor folded his arms about her, holding her close so that all she could do was lean against him and let out some of the pain and tension she'd been holding for the past days. All at once she sobbed uncontrollably as he held her, soothing her, gently stroking her back, her hair, before moving towards the big leather wing chair by the fire and placing her carefully in his lap.

It felt good, so wonderful, to be safe in his arms. For the moment she forgot all the doubts and fears of the past weeks, knew only that this was the one place she could find solace in her hour of need.

'It's all right, *querida*, I won't leave you,' he whispered, sensing her insecurity, her need to be cherished and taken care of.

Once she was able to speak, Araminta sat up on his knee and poured out all the pain of the stilted relationship with her mother during all these years, and the sudden unexpected reconciliation only days before her death. It had all happened so fast she could barely comprehend or make sense of it.

'The main thing is that it happened,' he told her, wiping her cheeks with his thumb before producing a large white handkerchief. 'Think of it as a gift that you were both given before it was too late. She left you with the knowledge that she did indeed love you, despite everything.'

Araminta nodded, laid her head on his shoulder and absorbed the warmth of him, the scent of him, the wonderful knowledge that he was here, next to her, when she most needed him.

Gently Victor kissed her lips, and Araminta felt her heart melt. For it was not a sensual kiss, but a deep, endearing gesture of—love. The knowledge shocked her into a sitting position. She was already so confused, the last thing she could deal with now was the realisation that she'd fallen madly in love with a married man. She would have to deal with it in the future, but right now all she could do was take what he offered.

Then suddenly she felt another surge of the nausea that had been bothering her for the past few days.

'Are you all right?' Victor asked, looking at her ashen face, worried. You don't look very well.'

'I don't feel very well,' she murmured, rushing from his knee and heading out of the room to the bathroom, where she retched. After several moments the feeling passed, and she took a sip of water before returning to the study where Victor was pacing the floor, his expression deeply worried.

'Araminta, *querida*, you're not well. You'd better see a doctor. I'll drive you immediately.'

'No, it's nothing—just nerves. I'll be fine.'

'Why don't you come and stay at the Manor?' he insisted. 'The press will be here as soon as this leaks out. I'll take you for a long ride on the Downs. The fresh air will do you good.'

'All right.' Araminta smiled up at him, knowing she couldn't leave him right now even if she tried. He took her hand in his, dark eyes gazing possessively down at her.

It was all she had right now, she realised, and Pearce had already warned her that journalists would soon be camping in front of Taverstock Hall. It would be much better to leave and feel protected by Victor's strong presence than stay here, fighting her battles alone.

CHAPTER THIRTEEN

THE next three days passed in a haze for Araminta. All she knew, during the funeral and afterwards, was that she never would have got through it if Victor had not been staunchly yet unobtrusively by her side, attentive to her every need, obstructing the path of obnoxious journalists and photographers who, with no respect for her grief, tried to corner her on the steps of the church, despite the cordoned-off area that the local police had carefully erected.

When she felt sick he held her over the basin; when she was tired he soothed her; when she needed to sleep he provided her with a soft pillow, then tucked her up in one of the guest bedrooms at the Manor, and stayed close to her until she fell fast asleep.

The night after the funeral Victor watched Araminta's exhausted eyelids close and sighed with relief. She'd been through so much during the past few days that he wondered how she'd held up. Especially as she'd hardly eaten a thing, saying that food made her feel sick.

Now, as he sat on the edge of the wide guest bed, he reached over and touched her golden hair with his fingertips.

She looked so frail, so young, almost like a child, lying there alone among the pillows. Gently, careful not to wake her, he eased himself onto the bed and lay quietly next to her. He would stay a little longer and make sure she didn't wake up screaming, as she had the previous night, woken by a nightmare. Leaning back, he rested his head against the pillows, realising that the strain of the past few days had rubbed off on him. And despite his efforts to stay awake soon his eyes too were closing, and he fell asleep, one hand reaching across Araminta's sleeping body.

Araminta dreamed now, her pain and exhaustion set aside for a few liberating hours. She dreamed of his arms coming around her, of his body close to hers. Stirring, she turned in her sleep and threw off the covers. Victor stirred too, and unconsciously drew her into his arms. Still half-asleep, Araminta snuggled closer, felt his hand close over her tummy. And somewhere, deep in her subconscious mind a new, mysterious and wonderful knowledge took root.

It was early when he woke and felt the warmth of her wrapped against him, provoking an immediate reaction. He tried to shift, but Araminta was closely cuddled up and it would have been impossible without waking her. When he felt her stir Victor let his hands glide down her body in a soothing, caressing gesture.

'Mmm. That feels so nice,' she murmured, shifting her head on the pillow and slipping her arms around his neck.

Unable to resist her tender, warm, sleepy gesture, Victor kissed her gently, let his mouth roam over her cheek, past her chin and down her throat. He felt her arch like a satisfied cat, and continued on down until his mouth reached the tip of her rose-nippled breast, where he stopped, hesitating for a moment lest she wake completely. But all she did was sigh, eyes still closed.

Unable to stop himself, Victor took the tip of her breast between his lips and taunted it slowly, lazily, while his hands wandered over her legs, edged up the silky texture of her nightgown and allowed his fingers to reach between her thighs to the mass of soft curls between them. She felt so warm, so liquid and pliable, that he reached further, his fingers seeking a pathway to the spot he knew rendered her senseless.

Araminta delighted in the feel of Victor's fingers, caressing her in places that sent incredible sensations rocketing through her, arrows of heat and desire into parts of her being that she'd never thought existed before he'd touched her. Then all at once her eyes opened and she came to, realising that this was no dream, but very real.

But it was too late to stop, too late to do more than submit to his expert caresses. When he entered her, gently, with a care hitherto unknown, she felt tears knotting her throat. There was something new, something deep and tender in this loving that hadn't existed previously, and which gave their coming together a new and profound dimension. He moved inside her as though wanting to reach the depths of her, to know each tiny part of her being until he reached her soul. And likewise Araminta opened up, seeking to take him deep within her, to feel this man as she had never felt any other.

She felt something stir in her tummy, knew a desire to cherish and protect, and wondered for a moment why she was feeling so tender. The fact that he was being so gentle, so caring and loving, made her want to cry as they came—not crashing, as they had before, or in a rush, but in a long, lingering flow, like gentle waves lapping the shore, over and over, until finally they lay in each other's arms with no need for words, no need for anything but the wonderful closeness they experienced in this most special of moments.

Dawn was breaking when they fell asleep again in each other's arms, only to wake at ten o'clock to rain pelting the window panes.

'Looks like a rotten day,' Victor murmured, smoothing her hair back before rising and parting the curtains.

'What day is it?' Araminta asked sleepily. She'd lost track of time and knew that however hard it was to focus she must get grip of reality.

'January the eighth,' he answered.

Araminta watched Victor dragging his fingers through his mussed hair. Had they really spent the night together once again? It seemed so natural, yet so strange that this man with whom she knew she only had a temporary relationship should have been here for her when she most needed someone. She could not have asked for a more loyal and faithful companion at her side, she reflected with a sigh. But now that the funeral was over she had to force herself to pick up the threads of her life.

Slowly Araminta sat up and drew away the covers, aware that her body felt warm and loved and wishing the sensation could go on for ever. Then suddenly she felt the familiar nausea growing steadily in her stomach.

'Oh, no, not again,' she begged, stumbling to the bathroom.

'What's the matter?' Victor followed her, concerned.

'I don't know what's wrong with me. I just feel so sick all the time—especially in the morning,' she wailed, holding the basin for support.

'I'll get Manuel to make you some tea,' Victor said, his brows creased with worry. 'Are you sure you'll be all right by yourself?'

'Fine,' she nodded, thankful to see him go.

After several moments the sensation subsided and she was able to lean back and sit on the edge of the bath. It must all be due to the nervous strain of losing her mother and knowing that in less than a week she had to face television interviews and newspaper reporters, go through all the press junkets that Pearce was setting up for her which couldn't be delayed.

She would just have to pull herself together and get on with it, she realised, letting out a little sigh, wishing she could open a hole in the ground and let it swallow her up.

And Victor?

What about Victor? He'd been so attentive, so caring and kind, with the result that she knew the wrench when it came would be doubly hard to deal with. How could she pretend she didn't care for him when her whole being cried out for his love?

Dropping her head in her hands, Araminta gave way to a moment of self-pity. It was so hard to know she'd found the man of her dreams but that this very man didn't want her the way she wanted him, too cruel that fate should have seen fit to place him in her path only to have him disappear as soon as things got back to normal. For that, she realised, rising stiffly from the edge of the bath, was exactly what would happen. Victor was here for her now because he knew she needed him, needed a friend in her moment of sadness. But after that it would be over.

Suddenly Araminta looked at herself in the mirror. She seemed abnormally pale. Well, that wasn't surprising after all she'd lived through during the past days. Again she felt dizzy, and moved into the bedroom, where she sat down in the armchair by the window, wishing she could just stay put for a little longer, not have to rush anywhere or be on show for anyone.

At that moment the door opened and Victor came in, carrying a tray piled with tea and cups and toast.

'Here,' he said, depositing it on the ottoman next to the chair. 'This should make you feel better. Probably haven't had enough to eat. I should think that's what's wrong with you, *querida*.'

'Probably,' Araminta agreed. 'Victor, I think I should go back to Taverstock Hall today. The press will have gone by now, and I need to make so many arrangements before I go to London.'

'I don't like the idea of you being there on your own,' he remarked, pouring a cup of tea and handing it to her. 'You should have someone there with you.'

'I'll ask Olive to sleep over. I'm sure she'll agree.'

'All right,' he conceded reluctantly, wishing she could stay but knowing that of course she was right. 'I'll drive you over later on.'

'Thank you,' she answered gratefully, taking a small sip of tea. 'You've been so wonderful to me these past few days, Victor. I don't know how I would have got through it without you.'

'Not at all,' he responded gruffly.

'No, I mean it.' She reached over and touched his hand, noticing how he tensed as she did so. Was he already regretting his overtures of friendliness? she wondered, sudden pain hurtling through her. Could it be that he was afraid she would interpret his gesture as meaning more than he'd promised?

Quickly Araminta withdrew her hand, determined to leave as soon as possible. 'I'll get showered and dressed, and then if you don't mind we'll go,' she said, laying her cup regretfully back in the saucer.

Victor looked at her for a minute, his face hard and taut, and she wondered what she'd said to cause this reaction.

'Okay,' he said at last. 'I'll leave you to get ready.' Then he rose and left the room without so much as a backwards glance.

Half an hour later Araminta was downstairs, thanking Manuel for all his kindness. The Brazilian manservant had been extremely solicitous, attending to her every need, and she felt grateful to him.

Then Victor picked up her tote bag and she followed him down the steps to the Range Rover.

It took only a few minutes to drive to Taverstock Hall, and Araminta found herself wishing the journey was longer. All at once they were back in that no-man's-land she'd lived through twice before, that dreadful blank nothingness, where feelings could no longer be expressed and only politeness remained. She felt hurt and stunted and— Oh, what did it matter what she felt? The sooner it was over the better.

When Victor drew up she jumped out quickly, holding her bag.

'Thanks for everything,' she said again as he came around the car. 'You've been a wonderful friend.' It seemed so inadequate to say this to a man whom she'd loved with more passion than she could have believed possible only hours earlier.

But so it was.

'Goodbye, Araminta. And please promise you won't disappear on me again?' His expression was dark, but it softened slightly at these words.

'No, I won't disappear,' she murmured. 'I'm renting a flat in London not far from you—in Wilton Crescent.'

'Good, then I shall expect to find you there.'

The authoritative tone was restored and she glanced at him, wondering what could be going on in his mind.

'Right. Well, I'll be seeing you, then,' she murmured awkwardly.

'I'll phone you tonight to make sure you're all right. I may have to pop up to London for a couple of days, but I'll be back by the weekend. If you need anything be sure to call Manuel. He'll take care of it for you.' He dropped a kiss on her brow and squeezed her arm.

Araminta watched as he climbed back into the car and drove slowly off down the drive, wondering if a heart could actually physically break. And knowing that if anybody's could it was hers.

CHAPTER FOURTEEN

FOR the next couple of days Araminta concentrated on dealing with all the practical matters pertaining to her mother's estate. She met with her lawyer, who read her the terms of the will. Everything had been left to her. Now she had to think what to do with Taverstock Hall. She loved the place dearly, for it reminded her of her childhood and her late father, and now of her mother as well. Well, there was no need to make any rushed decisions.

Olive came in and told her lunch was ready.

'Thanks, Olive, but I really don't think I—'

'Now, now, Miss Araminta, what's this nonsense about not eating?' she interrupted, placing her hands on her wide hips and shaking her permed grey head.

'I just feel so sick the whole time. Well, not the whole time, actually,' she said, tilting her head to one side. 'Just in the morning, really.'

'Is that so?' Olive peered at her, eyes narrowed, and drew her own conclusions. 'Have you seen the doctor?'

'No. I don't think I'm really ill—just a bit off-colour.'

'Have you thought that it might be something else?' Olive queried in her matter-of-fact manner.

'What do you mean?' Araminta looked up at her, eyes questioning.

'Well, now, Miss Araminta, I would have thought that a woman of your age would realise that it could be—you know—' Olive made an embarrassed gesture and Araminta stared at her, aghast, suddenly understanding the meaning of her words.

'Oh, my God,' she whispered. 'You mean I might be pregnant?'

'Well, there's no saying. These things do happen,' Olive muttered. And by the way Miss Araminta and the gentleman up at the Manor had been carrying on, close as Siamese twins, she wouldn't be in the least surprised.

'But that's awful.' Araminta gulped. 'I mean, not awful, it's wonderful as well, but, oh, Olive—' Suddenly she burst into a flood of tears, and Olive hurried over to the sofa.

Sitting next to Araminta, she put an arm around her and patted her shoulder. 'Now, now, don't get upset, dearie. If you are pregnant it'll do the baby no good. If I was you I'd pop down to the village and ask Dr Collins to do one of those newfangled pregnancy tests. My niece had one the other day. She knew at once. No waiting around for weeks, like in my day.'

'Do you think so?' Araminta asked doubtfully, scared of what the answer might be, an image of Victor flashing before her.

How could they have been so foolish as not to have taken any proper precautions?

What was she to do? In her heart of hearts, Araminta thought that she already knew the result of the test. Still, Olive was right. The best thing to do was make an appointment as soon as possible and find out the truth.

Next morning Araminta stepped out of Dr Collins's office into the blistering wind and shivered—not with cold but with emotion; she was expecting a baby.

Part of her was experiencing the thrill of knowing she was going to be a mother, the other, the part that knew she'd been thoroughly irresponsible, was in a tumult of confusion.

What would she tell Victor? she wondered as she walked down the street towards her car, parked in the same spot where she'd first run into him. She stood there a moment and stared. It seemed like many months ago, yet it wasn't that long.

Long enough to get pregnant, she rationalised, clicking open the car door and climbing in, more careful with her movements, as though she might harm the tiny bit of life throbbing inside her.

As she drove Araminta thought of all the possibilities open to her. She'd barely buried her mother, yet here she was expecting a baby. What would her mother have said, had she known? Araminta quailed at the thought. Would she have expected her to have an abortion? The thought left her trembling, and she almost had an accident as she turned a corner too abruptly, causing another car to veer perilously to the left.

All at once Araminta knew that whatever happened she was keeping this baby. After all, she didn't need Victor. Lots of women had babies on their own nowadays. What was the problem? She was financially independent, could provide for the child perfectly well without any help. So why was she so unhappy?

Back at the hall Araminta told Olive the truth, but begged her to remain silent on the subject. And, although she was bursting with excitement, Olive promised to keep her employer's secret.

The problem she faced now, Araminta realised glumly, was whether or not she should tell the child's father.

She spent the rest of the afternoon churning the problem over in her mind. Perhaps she wouldn't tell him right away. Perhaps she'd wait. But then what if he found out? How would he react? Would he want to be a part of the child's life even though he didn't want any long-term commitment with her? It was all so difficult and confusing, and in the end Araminta decided the best thing to do was leave before he returned and give herself some more time to think about it.

'You're what?' Pearce exclaimed, staring at her across the table at Mark's Club, wondering if he'd heard right.

'I told you, I'm expecting a baby,' Araminta answered in a low voice. 'Now, don't make a scene for goodness' sake. It's not a big deal.'

'Not a big deal?' Pearce spluttered. 'Araminta, are you aware of what a publicity coup this will be? When is it going to be born? In time to coincide with the next volume, I hope?' he said severely.

'Pearce, I did not get pregnant to oblige you or satisfy my fans,' she said, laughing despite her agitation. 'And, please, this is a secret. I only told you because I thought you should be aware of what was going on.'

'And who, may I ask, is the lucky father?'

'I don't want to talk about it,' she said, clamming up.

'Don't want—? But, Araminta, this is crazy. You sit down here, cool as a cucumber, and tell me you're expecting, and then don't want to tell me who the father is. Though I'd take a guess at it,' he said, eyeing her shrewdly.

'Really?' Araminta tried to sound nonchalant, but her colour was up and she swallowed tightly. Surely Pearce hadn't guessed that Victor was the one?

'Haven't you told him yet?' Pearce asked, taking a sip of his Buck's Fizz.

'No. No, I haven't.'

'May I ask why not?' he enquired severely. 'Doesn't he have a right to know?'

'Yes. No. I don't know.' Araminta lifted her glass and took a long sip of champagne, then remembered that she shouldn't be drinking.

'Araminta, are you telling me that you are expecting Victor's child and he knows nothing about it?'

She stared down at her hands, clasped in her lap, and nodded glumly.

'Well,' Pearce exclaimed, digesting the information, 'I think that's something you'd better remedy at once, old girl. If there's one thing the man loathes, it's being lied to.'

'I'm not lying. He might not want to know. After all, he's a married man, and may not want the responsibility of a child.'

'Who told you he was married?'

'He did.'

'I see.' Pearce frowned, trying to make head or tail of the situation. The last time he'd seen Victor he'd been anxious to reach Araminta and only too glad to tell him that his divorce had come through. None of this made any sense.

'Pearce, promise you won't say anything about this to Victor, or anyone else for that matter. I told you in the strictest confidence.'

'I'm aware of that. Still, it's my duty to advise you, as your friend—and as a friend of Victor's, I might add—that I think the only decent thing to do is to tell him the truth.'

'I'll think about it,' she conceded, then quickly changed the subject before he could go on questioning her.

'Aren't you going to invite me round to see your new place?' Victor asked, switching the cellphone to his other ear as he walked down Sloane Street, content with his purchase at Chanel—a handbag that for some reason he'd decided would be perfect for Araminta. 'I'm at a loose end right now and I have something I want to give you. Plus, I'm only a five-minute walk away.' He glanced at the black and white carrier bag and smiled, hoping she'd like it.

'Okay. Come over, if you like.'

'Try not to sound too enthusiastic,' he rejoined, laughing.

'Sorry, I'm a bit distracted, what with one thing and another. But come. I'll be waiting.'

'See you in ten minutes, then.'

What was she to do? Araminta wondered, her heart beating nineteen to the dozen. She slipped her hand protectively over her tummy. She simply couldn't tell him about the baby, not right now. For what if he reacted badly? What if he got cross and she got upset and—? Better not to think about it at all, just receive him normally and not let it worry her. There would be plenty of occasions further down the line when she could tell him, when the moment was right.

The sound of the doorbell had her hurrying to the front door.

'Hello.'

'Hello. Come in,' she said, forcing a bright, welcoming smile onto her face, and hoping the thud of her pulse could not be heard.

'This is for you.' Victor handed her the Chanel carrier bag, then slipped off his black cashmere coat.

'For me?' Araminta took the package and stared at it. Why was he giving her a present?

'Open it and see if you like it,' he said as they walked through into the living room. 'Nice place,' he murmured admiringly, taking in the pale lemon walls, the cream sofas and tasteful antiques.

'You shouldn't have brought me a gift,' Araminta said uncomfortably as she undid the ribbon, opened the box and removed the beautiful cream *matelassé* leather handbag—the one she'd been looking at only yesterday and had thought of buying.

'This is unbelievable!' she exclaimed, forgetting her worries for a moment in her delight. 'I saw this bag yesterday and thought of getting it. How did you guess? Thank you so much.' She leaned over to kiss him on the cheek. But Victor slipped his palm lightly against the back of her neck and drew her lips to his.

'I've missed you, *minha linda*, missed you more than I thought possible.'

'Victor, don't—' But her words were muted by his lips skimming hers, his tongue playing relentlessly, and the feel of his body pressed hard against her. She knew she must stop at once, knew she must not let him render her senseless, must keep her wits about her.

But it was impossible not to surrender to the insistence of his hands, moving so knowledgeably up and down her body, not to yearn for more than just his hard chest pressed against her already aching nipples. What did this man do to her? Why was it she could already feel herself melting inside? Feel herself going liquid at his touch? Feel her limbs weakening as she inhaled the scent of his aftershave, that unique scent that was his and his alone?

With a sigh Araminta dropped the handbag on the sofa and gave herself up to his embrace, knowing that in doing so she was only stepping in deeper. But there was simply nothing else she could do, no way she could resist. For a moment she wished she could pull back, tell him the truth, share this wondrous yet terrifying experience with him. But something stopped her and she gave way to his kisses, pushed the problem to the back of her mind and sank with him onto the couch.

If this was all she was going to be allowed then she would take it now and store the memories for the difficult days up ahead, when he probably wouldn't be about and she would have to face the future with her baby alone.

Victor drew back, caressed her cheek and frowned. 'Is something the matter, *querida*? You seem distracted.'

'No, I—' She couldn't go on, couldn't look into his eyes, see that searching yet autocratic look and not tell him the truth. Instead she buried her head in his shoulder and muffled the tears that were always so close to the surface these days.

'What is the matter?' he whispered, bringing his arms about her and holding her close as he caressed her back. 'Please tell me what is wrong. Is it your mother you're grieving for? Is that what is causing all this unhappiness?'

Araminta hesitated. It would be so easy to lie. Then she remembered Pearce's words at lunch. Bracing herself she drew back and got up from the sofa while Victor watched her, his dark brows coming together in a thick line above the bridge of his patrician nose.

'What is it, Araminta? You look very worried and upset. Tell me,' he ordered.

She moved closer to the window, looked out a moment, then swallowed and turned to face him.

'Something's happened, Victor. I—' She felt desperate, looking at him with fearful eyes, watching as he rose from the sofa and seeing his face close.

'What is it?' he asked harshly, a sinking sensation gripping him.

He should have known it was too good to last. His mind ran back over what Pearce had told him. Of course—she'd found another man when she'd been away in the Caribbean! How could he have been such a fool? Isabella had always shown him what women were capable of. While he had been sitting waiting like an idiot in Eaton Place, Araminta had obviously been up to other things.

More fool him.

'Victor, I need to tell you this before things get any more complicated between us.'

'Don't bother,' he retorted forcefully, his face set in hard taut lines, his memory held fast by another, past and devastating betrayal. 'I can guess. Well, it was good while it lasted, Araminta. I knew, of course, that it was only a passing fling, which is why I didn't bother to become emotionally involved. So much easier this way, don't you think?' He laughed, a short, harsh laugh that left her in no doubt as to his feelings. 'Look, I'd better dash now,' he said, glancing at his watch. 'I'll see you around some time. No need to see me to the door.'

Araminta stayed glued to the spot while he turned on his heel and marched out into the hall. She wanted to run after him, plead with him, tell him to wait, that she needed to explain. What had he guessed? she wondered. Had he realised what she was about to tell him, that she was expecting his baby? Or had he understood something completely different? Why had he reacted so angrily?

Desperate, she sank into the nearest chair and dropped her head in her hands. This was it. It was over. Any hopes she'd had were dead. There was nothing for it but to face the future alone and make sure her baby was loved and provided for, even if it didn't have a father.

She sat up then, determined not to give way to her emotions. It wasn't good for the baby, and that was her uppermost priority now. She would not allow anyone or anything, least of all Victor and his selfish arrogance, to harm her child.

Araminta rose and stared for a moment at the bag lying on the sofa next to the box and the tissue paper. She would probably never use it now she realised with an anguished sigh, never look at it. For it marked a turning point in her life, a milestone that she would never forget for as long as she lived.

Victor left Wilton Crescent furious and walked the rest of the way to Eaton Place trying to understand why Araminta's feckless behaviour—which, of course, he'd expected all along—should have left him so entirely undone and upset.

Damn her.

Damn all women.

Why was he a sentimental fool? Why had he believed, during those days spent at the Manor after her mother's death, that things between them had developed into something deeper—something that, even though he had been loath to admit it, he craved?

And now, as always, came the reality check.

Well, so much the better. The last thing he needed was another ride on the emotional rollercoaster.

He let himself into the apartment and went immediately to the living room, where he poured himself a stiff whisky and stared into space, seeing her face before him and wishing he'd never laid eyes on it. He would sell the Manor, he decided abruptly. Get rid of the place and not be subjected to the possibility of running into her.

At that moment the ring of the phone brought him back to earth.

'Hello?' he answered tersely.

'Hello, old chap, it's me—Pearce.'

'Hi, what can I do for you?'

'You sound a bit down at the mouth, old chap. Everything okay?'

'Fine. What is it that you want?' Victor snapped.

'Well, actually, I was wondering if you'd like to have a bite of dinner somewhere. But of course if you're not in the mood we'll do it some other time.'

Victor hesitated. He didn't want anything right now. Then suddenly he changed his mind. What was the point of sitting here staring into space, making a bloody fool of himself? 'That's a good idea,' he replied. 'I'll meet you at Green's at eight.'

'Looking forward to it.'

Pearce hung up the phone and grimaced. Something was definitely wrong, and it didn't take a rocket scientist to tell him it had to do with Araminta. He let out a long breath. He was going to have to do something about those two. He simply couldn't allow things to deteriorate. After all his own future was at stake, he reasoned. Araminta might suddenly decide not to write any more books.

And then where would they all be?

CHAPTER FIFTEEN

'How about a bottle of Pouilly Fuissé,' Pearce murmured, glancing over the wine menu. 'You look as if you could do with a drink.'

'I most certainly could,' Victor agreed. He'd simmered down somewhat in the past few hours, but the indignation, humiliation and bitter anger still lingered.

Pearce ordered the wine and settled back in the booth, looking his friend over. Victor's dark features looked stormy, and he wondered if Araminta had summoned up her courage and this was the result.

'I had lunch with Araminta today,' he remarked, deciding to plunge in at the deep end.

'Did you, now?' The twist of the other man's mouth became cynical and he smiled, a harsh, unamused smile. 'Quite a little number, your friend Araminta.'

'*My* friend?'

'Well, isn't she?'

'Yes, I suppose she is.'

'Why didn't you tell me she had it off with some chap in Barbados?' Victor threw in suddenly, unable to suppress his anger. Damn Pearce. He was an accomplice, after all.

'Excuse me?' Pearce drew his brows together and sent his friend a haughty look. 'I have no idea what you're talking about.'

'Come on, Pearce, surely you have some loyalty to me, despite your commercial interest in Araminta,' Victor muttered bitterly.

'I'm afraid you're going to have to be a little more explicit,' Pearce replied coldly, nodding to the wine waiter, who was ready to pour. 'I have no idea what you're talking about.'

Victor waited impatiently while the sommelier poured the wine and Pearce tasted it and approved. Finally the ritual was over and he leaned across the table.

'She told me this afternoon—or rather tried to confess. But I didn't give her the chance,' he added, with a mirthless laugh.

'Let me get this straight,' Pearce said slowly. 'You saw Araminta this afternoon and she tried to tell you something?'

'Yes. It can only be that she had an affair with another man while she was away celebrating the New Year.'

'And what makes you so sure of that?'

'Well, what else could it be?' Victor exclaimed, taking a long sip of wine. 'What else could make a woman pull back, stand there fidgeting, clasping her hands, saying she has something to tell me and looking guilty as sin?' he enquired, with a sarcastic lift of his brow.

'Personally, I can think of a number of things,' Pearce replied dryly. 'Don't you think that perhaps you've been a bit hasty?'

'I don't see why,' Victor responded, suddenly less sure of himself. 'It was obvious.'

'Perhaps not,' Pearce answered, looking him straight in the eye.

'What makes you say that?' Victor pounced, attentive all at once.

'I'm afraid I'm not at liberty to say.'

'To hell with all this subterfuge. Just tell me.'

'I'm sorry, old chap, but I'm afraid it's not my place.'

'Look, don't start this cat and mouse business all over again,' Victor ground out. 'It's Araminta we're talking about here. I thought she was different. I was imbecile enough to believe that maybe—' He cut himself off, realising what he was admitting, and bit back the words that he didn't want to hear himself, let alone tell another.

'That you're in love with her?' Pearce asked softly.

'Of course I'm not in love with her, that's perfectly ridiculous. It's just that—'

'Why don't you admit it, Victor?' Pearce laid his glass down and looked his friend straight in the eye. 'My advice to you, old chap, is to go back to Araminta and ask her exactly what it was she wanted to tell you this afternoon. And don't go there looking like a bad-tempered bear or she'll kick you out, lock, stock and barrel, and you'll get no sympathy from me.'

'You know something—' Victor controlled his temper with difficulty. Then, throwing down his napkin, he rose. 'I'm not standing for this a moment longer. I'm going there to clear this whole thing up right now.'

'An excellent idea, old chap.' Pearce raised his glass and watched him leave with a smile. Those two really were made for each other, he concluded, taking another long sip of deliciously cold wine. He just hoped that now they might finally manage to sort themselves out.

With a sigh he resigned himself to a solitary dinner, content in the knowledge that he'd done all he could to right matters.

Victor's temper was not improved by the time he'd searched vainly for a parking place in Wilton Crescent. In the end he valet-parked the Bentley at the Berkeley Hotel and took the few steps over to Araminta's. What was the matter with her? If it wasn't another man, then why had she looked so guilty, so self-conscious?

Two minutes later he rang the doorbell and waited. She'd damn well better be in, or he'd be left feeling even more frustrated than he already was. Tapping his fingers impatiently on the doorknob, he waited. Then the intercom hissed and with relief he heard her voice.

'Araminta, it's me—Victor. I need to talk to you.'

There was a moment's hesitation. 'I don't think there's anything left to say.'

'Look, please—I'm sorry I was so abrupt this afternoon. We need to talk.'

'I don't think so.'

'Araminta, I'm warning you, if you don't let me in I'll break down the door and cause a hell of a fuss out here. Is that clear?'

He really was impossible, Araminta reflected in silent outrage as she crossly pressed the release button for him to enter. Why should she be subjected to his tyrannical behaviour? Wasn't it enough that he'd walked out?

With a resigned sigh she went to the door, prepared to face the storm. Now that she'd made up her mind to assume her responsibilities she wasn't frightened any more, and knew exactly what she had to do. She would listen to what he had to say, then get rid of him once and for all and put an end to this whole wretched nonsense.

The knot in her throat tightened. She touched her belly protectively as she heard the elevator come to a stop on the landing. Then, swallowing, she pulled back her shoulders, glanced at herself in the mirror and, head high, went to open the door. Thank goodness she was wearing a soft white cashmere sweater and skirt and didn't look a frump.

She simply couldn't have borne facing him without the right armour.

She looked too beautiful for words! Victor swallowed, standing uncomfortably on the threshold.

'Come in,' Araminta said, turning and moving regally towards the drawing room, where a fire was lit and the room shimmered softly in the lamplight. Somehow she looked even lovelier than he'd remembered her, almost ethereal as she sat down next to the fire.

'I won't offer you a drink,' she said coldly, 'as I presume what you have to say won't take long.'

'Actually, if you don't mind, I could use one,' he said ruefully.

'Then be my guest.' She pointed to an antique lowboy on which a tray with decanters and tumblers stood. Victor moved towards it slowly, giving himself time as he poured himself a whisky.

'Can I get you anything?' he asked.

'No, thank you.'

It wasn't so easy now he was actually here to broach the subject, when she was seated so cool, calm and collected. Suddenly everything that earlier had seemed so clear and which he'd been so sure of didn't seem quite so etched in stone.

'Look, I came back because I think I was rather hasty this afternoon,' he said, raising his glass and taking a sip, eyeing her carefully over the rim of the tumbler, a sudden pang of desire shooting through him.

'I don't know why you bothered,' she murmured. 'You appeared very sure of your actions.'

'Did I?' he asked, eyes narrowing.

'Well, you made it abundantly clear what kind of opinion you hold of our relationship, so I really don't think there's very much else to be said.'

'Look, I'm sorry. I may have made a mistake. I'm afraid I've become rather cynical over the years. Things have happened in my life which make it hard for me to trust in others.'

'What a shame,' she said in a languid voice.

'Yes. Actually, it is. I see that myself now. Look, Araminta, when you began telling me something this afternoon, I thought you were trying to tell me you'd been with another man.'

'And why was that suddenly so important? After all, we have no commitment.'

'I know, but—'

'No,' she interrupted, getting up, her eyes suddenly blazing with anger. 'You are the one who said you couldn't commit. *Let's live the moment* were your very words. If I had gone off with somebody else it would have served you right.'

They were facing each other now, Araminta stormy-eyed, Victor watching her warily, enchanted by this flaring attack that told him all he needed to know.

She had not been unfaithful to him, her anger proved it.

'Look, *querida*, I'm sorry.' He moved towards her. 'Can't we forget this and start over?'

'Start over? No. I don't think so. The way you've behaved is appalling. I've had enough. I don't want to see you ever again.' Tears were swimming in her eyes as she spoke.

'But, Araminta, darling, you must understand. This is far more serious than I believed. I've just realised how much I feel for you and that—'

'Oh, have you?' she raged furiously. 'Well, it's too late, Victor Santander. You should have thought of this before. And you're married, so there's no future for us anyway.'

'If you'll let me explain—'

'What is there to explain?' she threw, hot tears pouring down her cheeks. 'Married is married, and there are no half measures about it. I got a letter from your wife,' she added bitterly, 'with pictures of both of you together. I've been a fool, and wrong to have let you anywhere near me after that.'

'What do you mean, a letter?' He frowned angrily. Isabella was up to her old tricks.

'Exactly that.'

'When?'

'After I got back from Barbados. Look, can't we just drop this whole thing? You go your way, I go mine? This whole discussion is pointless.'

'Araminta, please, give me a chance to explain,' Victor begged, moving forward and grabbing her arms. 'I'm not married to Isabella any longer. I got divorced when I was in Brazil, that's why the trip took me so long and why I didn't get in touch. I was tying up all the loose ends.'

Araminta stood perfectly still in his grip and stared at him. 'Divorced?' she whispered, unable to believe her ears.

'Yes, divorced.'

'Why didn't you tell me?' she bristled, a cold fury rising within her as full realisation heaped on her. He'd allowed her to go on thinking he was married, deluded her so that she wouldn't ask for anything, wouldn't expect any commitment from him. In other words he didn't trust her.

All at once she tore from his arms in pain and rushed to the window. 'Get out of my house,' she hissed, trembling, unable to control her intense hurt any longer. 'Get out of here and never come back. I think you're utterly despicable. And I never want to see you again. Ever.'

Then she turned and ran from the room, slamming the door behind her.

Victor stood staring at the door, assimilating all that had just transpired. She was deeply hurt, that much was obvious, and apparently all his suspicions had been unfounded. Then what was it that she'd been trying to tell him earlier?

Dragging his fingers through his thick black hair, Victor stared at the pattern of the oriental rug beneath his feet and tried to analyse the situation. What could have made her look so guilty, so confused and embarrassed?

For a moment he gazed at the door, inclined to follow her, insist that she tell him the truth, whatever it was. But he hesitated. She'd been through so much lately, what with her mother's death, the excitement of the book, and not least what he himself had put her through. He felt ashamed of his own precipitous conclusions. It just went to prove how cynical and hard-bitten he'd become, how the events of the past few years had marked him.

All at once he looked up and his eyes fell upon a picture of Araminta in a silver photo frame. She was seated cross-legged, staring out at the sea, in a typical pose of hers. His mouth softened, his eyes lingered, and he realised for the first time just how much this woman had come to mean to him, how much she'd changed him. Should he go in there and seek her out? Or give it a little time to let the dust settle?

Reluctantly he decided on the latter course. She was too upset right now. It would serve no purpose to harangue her. Better to allow her to rest and try again in the morning once they'd both calmed down and had time to think. He didn't take seriously her intimation of never wanting to see him again; that was an empty threat, he reasoned. But in the back of his mind a niggling sensation told him it might just be true.

All at once he decided he wasn't going any-where. He would stay here and sleep on the couch. That way she couldn't escape him even if she wanted to.

Araminta threw herself onto the bed and let go the flood of stifling tears. She could bear it no longer. Thank goodness she'd finally told him to leave and never come back. The deed was done and there was no going back on it. She wept bitter tears of pain, hunger, anguish, anger and remorse.

After a while the sobbing subsided and she pulled herself up into a sitting position and forced herself to think straight. She could not get into this emotional state. It might affect the baby. She could feel shooting pains in her abdomen and became afraid. Carefully she shifted her position, lay back against the pillows, breathing deeply, and drank some water from the Evian bottle next to her bed.

Little by little she regained her composure, but still her heart felt shattered to smithereens. The future seemed so bleak now, despite the baby and the pleasure she knew it would bring into her life. But it was *his* baby, *his* blood, and she was sure that it would be a little boy, and look just like Victor, with thick black hair and perfect features, reminding her at every turn of just how much she missed him.

Slowly she got up and forced herself to undress. She slipped on a pale pink silk spaghetti-strap negligée and, too tired to do more than clean her face and brush her teeth, collapsed into bed and turned off the light.

Maybe she'd be lucky and fall asleep, and forget this whole mess for a few glorious hours.

CHAPTER SIXTEEN

AT THREE a.m. Araminta woke up to rattling windows and slashing rain. She shivered and switched on the light. It must be a winter storm hitting London. She rubbed her eyes and, still shivering, reached for her dressing gown, remembering all at once that in her tempestuous state last night she'd forgotten to secure the front door.

Donning her slippers, she padded out of the bedroom and made her way down the passage into the hall to check the front door, frowning when she realised it had been locked. She turned and moved into the drawing room, where one lamp remained lit. Surely she hadn't had time to turn off all the lights?

The wind was stronger and the rain beating harder as she entered the room. She hated storms. Araminta felt suddenly fearful and alone, she and the tiny being alive inside her. Wrapping her arms around her, she moved further into the room. Then a movement from the couch made her gasp and stand frozen to the spot.

Somebody was in the flat, in this room. What was she to do? Terrified, Araminta knew she must protect her baby and herself from the invader.

Victor turned on the sofa, trying to find a comfortable position and failing to do so. Then he heard a noise and sat up. He looked towards the door and saw Araminta standing rigid as a statue in the doorway, her face white and terrified.

Leaping up, he moved across the room in two masterful strides.

'Why did you get up? Are you okay?' His brows creased in concern.

'Wh-what are you doing here?' she whispered, staring at him, limbs weak, as slowly she released the fear that had gripped her.

'Come over here and sit down.' Victor grabbed her arm and steadied her as, shaking, Araminta moved towards the couch.

'What are you doing here?' she asked again, bewildered yet desperately thankful that she wasn't alone, that there was no intruder, that although she'd told him to leave Victor had stayed.

'I didn't want to leave you alone,' he answered, lowering her to the cushions and wondering if she wasn't feeling well, for she had her right hand clamped over her stomach. 'Are you feeling all right?' he queried, standing over her, his face set in hard, worried lines. She looked so pale, so fragile. 'I'll get you a brandy.'

'No—please, I can't,' she murmured automatically.

'Rubbish, *querida*. Of course you can,' he replied briskly, 'it'll do you good.'

'No—no alcohol.'

'Araminta, don't be silly,' he said, touching her hair with his fingertips. 'Brandy will help revive you.'

'But I can't drink right now,' she murmured, leaning back and letting her head rest against the cushions, too tired to measure her words.

'Why not?' Victor asked peremptorily.

'Because I'm—'

Suddenly the full implication of what she was about to say hit her full in the gut and she sat up straight, face pale and hands shaking.

'Look, please, just leave me alone. I'll have a glass of water.'

'Araminta, I demand that you tell me immediately why you can't drink alcohol,' Victor commanded, his voice low and determined, his eyes narrowed as he surveyed her pale cheeks, turning suddenly rosy.

'It's not important,' she muttered, trying to stave him off. She couldn't—mustn't tell him.

'Araminta, don't lie to me. I hate lies. Tell me the truth at once.' He stood over her, eyes boring relentlessly into hers, allowing for no escape.

What was she to do? For a moment Araminta thought of denying the truth, then a wave of anguish swept over her and she knew she couldn't. For better or worse, she was going to have to admit reality.

'Well?' His features were hard and demanding, his mouth a thin line of determined expectation.

'I—I'm expecting a baby,' she whispered, holding his eyes for a moment, then lowering them to her hands, clasped nervously in her lap, as she waited for the storm she was sure would break over her head.

Stunned, Victor stood for a long moment absorbing the words. She was pregnant, was going to have a baby. So he'd been right after all.

The treachery of it seemed so intense, so vile. He swallowed, trying desperately to master his anger, his boiling rage at the thought of her *carrying another man's child.*

How could she have done this to him?

Araminta looked up at him warily. 'I know that we should have taken precautions. It's just that I haven't had a relationship since Peter died, and as he couldn't have children—well, I'd got used to never worrying about contraceptives. I don't expect you to assume any responsibility,' she continued nervously. 'It's my baby. I'll deal with the consequences.' She raised her proud chin a fraction, determined to be brave. 'You'll not have to worry about anything,' she murmured, unable to keep the bitterness from her voice.

Victor stared at her, unbelieving, the realisation of what she was saying dawning on him at last. It was *his* baby she was carrying, *his* child. Not some other man's but the fruit of their—love. The word hit him like an inside curve ball. Never, in all his years as a grown man, had anything affected him as Araminta's last few words.

'Araminta,' he whispered hoarsely, needing to confirm the truth, 'are you telling me we're going to have a baby?'

'No,' she said, rising, feeling far more in control now that the truth was aired and she'd accepted reality for what it was. '*I'm* having a baby.'

'*Our* baby,' he insisted, shoving his hands into the pockets of his grey pants, caught in a myriad of emotions he could hardly define.

'Victor, there is no need to get dramatic about this. *I* assume the responsibility. I'm perfectly able to provide financially for the child. Neither of us will be a burden on you,' she said, her head high.

'A burden?' he repeated, mystified. What was she talking about?

'Yes. I will register the baby in my name, that way it will cause you no embarrassment.' She looked him straight in the eye and took several steps back, then turned and hid the mounting tears, staring out of the window at the slashing rain, barely aware now of the howling wind, her pain was so great.

Victor watched her, wanting to react and unable to. Then all at once the full implication of her words hit him. His face turned dark with fury and he crossed the room and gripped her shoulders mercilessly. 'How dare you?' he demanded, his eyes flashing arrows. 'How dare you say these things?'

'What things?' Araminta trembled at the sight of his anger. It was worse than she'd believed. 'Please,' she said, suddenly frightened, 'don't be angry. It makes me so nervous, and that's not good for the baby.'

Victor gazed down at his hands, gripping her shoulders, and immediately let go. 'I'm sorry,' he said stiffly. 'I had no intention of harming you. Araminta, when did this happen? How long have you known? Why didn't you tell me before?' All at once a thousand questions poured from his lips. 'Why didn't you tell me at once?'

'Because I knew it would be a problem for you and I didn't know how you'd react,' she murmured, trying to be sensible, to ignore the torture that knowing he didn't care had caused.

'A problem? What the hell are you talking about? What kind of a man do you think I am?' he threw.

'I—'

'You had no right to keep this from me, to deny me this knowledge. You should have told me immediately—shared this news with me. I—I can't believe it,' he said, shaking his head, his expression changing to one of bewildered delight. 'You're carrying my child. But are you all right? You should be resting.'

To Araminta's amazement he slipped his arms under her and lifted her into them. '*Minha linda*, my beautiful Araminta. Let me lay you down somewhere. You must not be upset by anything, must not go anywhere,' he said in a masterful tone, laying her tenderly onto the couch.

'But—' Araminta blinked as he dropped a gentle kiss on her forehead and wrapped the throw around her.

'You must keep warm, you and the baby.'

'You—you mean you're not upset?' she whispered, staring up at him, unbelieving.

'Upset? Of course I'm not upset. It will be a boy, of course. My first son. Now, let me think. We must get married immediately.'

'But that's absurd, Victor,' she protested, struggling to a sitting position. 'I don't think you've thought this out properly. Please don't say things you don't mean.' The pain of hearing him fantasize left her with tears in her eyes. Perhaps to him this was all just a game, an amusing sideshow.

Victor looked down at her and gripped her hands in his. 'I do mean it. I am divorced now.'

'But you said when you left for Brazil that you had to see your wife. I don't understand any of this.'

'Yes. At that time I was separated from Isabella.' His face hardened. 'She was up to her tricks again, trying to stop me from divorcing her. But I was able to convince the judge and I got the decree. It's over. She will no more torment my life.'

'I see.' Araminta let out a tiny sigh, her relief and joy at his words tempered by common sense and what she knew she must say. 'But that doesn't necessarily mean that you want to get remarried so soon.'

'We are going to have a baby, Araminta. Of course we'll be married at once.'

'But this isn't the Middle Ages, Victor. People have babies without being married all the time.'

'Not in my book they don't,' he answered autocratically. 'We shall be married as soon as we can.'

'Might I point out,' she murmured, a little smile twitching the edges of her mouth, 'that you haven't asked me yet?'

'Haven't asked you? What do you mean?' He raised an astonished, uncomprehending brow.

'Exactly that. You haven't proposed.'

Victor stared down at her, flabbergasted. 'You mean you don't want to marry me?' he asked.

'I never said that. I just pointed out that I haven't been asked. Plus, I think I'd like a little time to think about it.'

'But this is ridiculous,' he exploded, letting go her hands and staring down at her in astonished outrage. 'Here I am, proposing to do the right thing by you, and you react in this absurd manner.'

'It's not absurd, merely realistic. I don't need any favours or to be dictated to,' she said haughtily, aware all at once that she was not going to be ordered about by him or anyone. 'I don't want to marry you just because I'm pregnant and you feel some old-fashioned need to prove you're an honourable gentleman. No, thanks.'

'Well!' Victor exploded, moving away, his mind in turmoil. 'If that's how you feel then there is really very little left to say. I think you are being ridiculous, childish, irresponsible and, I might add, selfish. I shall leave you to come to your senses,' he said, in a tone of umbrage, anger and pride battling as he refused to admit that the carpet had been neatly pulled from under his feet.

'You can't go out in this weather,' Araminta exclaimed. 'It's pouring cats and dogs.'

'I wouldn't give a damn if there was a force ten hurricane blowing,' he retorted. 'I'm out of here.'

'Well, it's entirely up to you.' She shrugged, a tiny smile dimpling her cheeks at the sight of him so flustered just because he wasn't getting his own way.

'I shall call in tomorrow and make sure you're in good health,' he announced coldly, putting on his coat. 'I want you to go straight to bed. You should not be up and about. If nothing else I insist that you take proper care of my child.'

With that he turned on his heel and stalked out of the apartment, leaving Araminta on the sofa, sadly wondering if she'd been too hasty in her response. But she knew she was right. Unless it was the real thing, unless he truly loved her as much as she loved him, there would be no hope for a marriage based on obligation.

It was all or nothing.

This time, she knew, she couldn't deal with anything less.

CHAPTER SEVENTEEN

'AND that's not all,' Victor pointed out, full of righteous indignation. 'Can you believe that she refused to marry me?' he exploded, leaning over Pearce's desk.

'Well, this is quite a turn of events,' Pearce muttered thoughtfully, watching his friend rise and pace the floor like a caged tiger. 'How did you put it to her?'

'As soon as I knew the truth I told her we would be married at once, of course. It was the obvious step to take. What else was I expected to have said?' He threw up his arms in despair. 'It's clearly the right solution.'

'Hmm. But Araminta doesn't agree, you say?'

'No. She must be mad. Do you know what she said?' he added, whirling round and slamming his hands on the desk.

'No, but I'm sure you're about to tell me,' Pearce murmured patiently.

'She said—' Victor pronounced the words with cold fury '—that I hadn't asked her. I don't understand.'

'Well, had you?'

'Had I what?'

'Asked her?'

'I just told you,' he reiterated impatiently. 'I made it quite clear that we'd be married right away.'

'Victor, I was referring to the verb *ask*, as in *solicit the co-operation of the other party*. Did you *ask* her? Or did you just *tell* her?' Pearce twiddled his gold pen and waited.

'What does it matter? It's all the same thing.' Victor dismissed the question with an autocratic gesture.

'I don't think so.'

'You don't think what?' he asked, bewildered.

'That it's the same thing.'

'Why on earth not? The result is the same, isn't it?'

'Not really. From what I'm gathering, Araminta believes you merely want to marry her to do your duty by the child—give it a name and so on.'

'Well? Isn't that a good enough reason?'

'Not any more. Women want to be loved for themselves. Having a child out of wedlock is not a big deal these days. Araminta needs to know that you love her.'

Victor stopped dead in front of Pearce's desk and frowned. 'But that should be self-evident,' he said with a half-laugh, lifting his hands in a gesture of incomprehension.

'Apparently not,' Pearce murmured dryly. 'Perhaps you should start working on a practical demonstration. Now, if you'll excuse me, old chap, I've got a pile of work to get through before lunch.'

Four days had passed and not a word from Victor.

Perhaps he'd regretted his hasty offer of marriage, had thought about her words and decided that she was right. Well, if that was the case it was certainly better to get it straightened out now rather than later. The last thing she wanted was a short, unhappy marriage that could only end in pain for all three of them. For now it was not just she and Victor she had to think about, but the baby too.

Araminta sighed, smothered the dull pain that hovered permanently below the surface, knowing she'd have to get used to it, and went about her business. Today she was having lunch with Pearce, to finalise her schedule for the interviews that would be taking place the week after next, and she must start thinking about contacting a nanny agency. Apparently they got booked up very quickly, and nannies needed to be reserved months before the birth.

As she was getting ready to go out the doorbell rang. Araminta moved towards the door, stifling the ever-present tiny hope that perhaps it might be Victor and that— But, no. It was a courier service and her heart sank.

'Thank you.' She smiled at the delivery man and looked down at the letter. Probably something to do with her new book contract.

With a sigh, she went into the drawing room and was about to lay the large envelope down on her desk and leave it until later when she frowned. She really must learn to be more businesslike and attend to these things immediately. After all, it might be something urgent that needed a signature. She could discuss it with Pearce over lunch.

Slitting open the large cardboard cover, Araminta removed a handwritten envelope from inside. And all at once her heart leaped.

It was Victor's writing. Fingers trembling, she opened it and unfolded the letter.

Dear Araminta,
After much reflection, I agree that this whole matter must be discussed carefully before any final decisions can be made. Therefore, I am inviting you to join me this weekend in the hope that we can pursue further discussion in an adult and sensible manner. My plane is at your disposal. If these arrangements are agreeable to you please contact Captain Ferguson at the following number. He awaits your instructions at your earliest convenience.

Victor

Araminta sank onto the desk chair and read the missive over twice, her heart heavy. So he had thought better of it after all, had realised that getting married for all the wrong reasons held no purpose. Bravely she swallowed. She might as well go and have it out with him. They would have to maintain a civilised relationship for the child's sake, so the sooner she got used to it the better. Today was Thursday, and she had nothing to do over the weekend anyway.

But there was no mention of where he wanted her to join him.

Typical, she reflected, letting out a sigh. Well, she'd find out soon enough. Perhaps it would be better to settle the future on neutral territory rather than in her house or in Sussex, where they'd lived through so many emotions. Picking up the phone, Araminta rang the plane's captain and told him she'd be ready to leave at four o'clock the next day. It was only when she laid down the receiver that she realised she'd forgotten to ask where they were flying to.

She was being flown to Normandy.

Araminta sat in the luxurious white leather seat of the Gulfstream and swallowed. Why did he want her to come to the spot where, according to the time-frame, she was certain the baby had been conceived? It seemed too cruel when he had obviously changed his mind and wanted nothing but a civilised adult relationship. He would probably insist on maintaining the child—might want some visiting rights.

She sighed and sipped the mineral water the steward had brought her, and watched a freighter navigating the English Channel below. At least after they'd settled things the situation would be clear-cut. There would be no more hoping, no more illusions, no room for any regrets.

There had been moments over the past few days when she'd questioned herself, wondered if she should have been less radically opposed to his proposal of marriage. But then she'd remembered his reaction, his need to be implicitly obeyed without dispute. And of course the formal wording of the note inviting her for the weekend told its own tale.

He had only spoken out of pride and a sense of duty, nothing more. His words had been uttered on the spur of the moment and were nothing more than a desire to find a practical solution to what he considered to be a problem.

And that she could never have borne.

Several minutes later the plane began its descent, and soon they were landing in Deauville. Araminta picked up her overnight bag—she didn't intend to stay more than one night—and stepped out of the aircraft, surprised and not a little disappointed to see no sign of Victor. The Aston Martin and the same chauffeur who'd driven them in London were waiting instead. She masked her regret, reasoning that it was better this way, and, smiling, climbed into the back of the car.

It was only after half an hour's drive that she became aware that instead of entering the historic town of Falaise they were entering the gates of the lovely château where Victor had taken her to see the horses. She sat up, brows creased, as the car glided up the drive and they stopped in front of the exquisite building, lit up like a fairy castle in the wintry mist.

The car came to a halt and the chauffeur opened the door and took her bag. Next thing she knew the doors were being flung open and a housekeeper was ushering her inside. The place was beautiful, she realised, looking about her at the black and white marble hall, the Louis XVI table decked with a magnificent flower arrangement under a sparkling eighteenth-century chandelier.

Why had he brought her here instead of to Le Moulin? she wondered, following the housekeeper up the wide staircase. And where was Victor? There had been no sign of him since her arrival. Perhaps he was too busy and only planned to spend the minimum time necessary in her company.

The housekeeper, a grey-haired woman with a pleasant smile, opened a wide door off the carpeted corridor and Araminta stepped inside a little salon, off which was a bedroom suite. It was charmingly decorated—very French, in creams and gold, but not too gilded or ornate. She loved the striped brocade curtains that brightened the room, and the little fireplace where logs crackled and by which a small sofa with plumped cushions looked comfy and inviting. And on the antique tables were cut-crystal vases filled with fresh flowers, brightening the winter's night.

The bedroom too was delightful, and as Araminta stepped inside it she was surprised to see a huge package lying on the bed. Intrigued, she moved towards it and frowned. What did this signify? She picked up a white envelope with her name written on it in Victor's inimitable hand, and her heart raced despite her desire to stay utterly cool. She opened it and read.

I shall expect you downstairs at eight. Dinner is formal.

Victor

Well. Araminta let out an annoyed breath and threw the note on the night table. He certainly didn't mince his words. And how was she expected to know that he was having a formal dinner party on the night of her arrival? This was hardly an occasion to be having guests over. In fact very much the contrary. He could at least have warned her. Now what was she going to wear?

Just as her anger against Victor was steadily mounting Araminta glanced again at the huge box on the bed. Hesitating, she opened it. And, to her surprise, from inside a sea of tissue paper she removed a gorgeous black and silver designer evening dress. The soft rich fabric moulded the curves of her body as she placed it against her and looked at herself in the mirror, realising it would be perfect. Then, looking again in the box, she saw a pair of exquisite black satin and diamanté evening shoes, and a matching clutch purse.

Was there anything the man hadn't thought of? she wondered, staring at the things, wishing suddenly that she didn't need them and could fling them back in his face with a proud refusal to accept. But then what would she wear?

Araminta let out a long, frustrated sigh and sat down crossly on the bed. She really didn't have much choice. It was wear the outfit or go to dinner in sporty trousers and a jacket.

She glanced at her watch and realised that it was already seven o'clock. After laying the clothes carefully back on the bed, she entered the huge marble and mirrored bathroom. She turned on the taps of a gloriously voluminous tub, added some delicious smelling bath lotion and began to undress. As she did so she observed herself in the mirror, noticing for the first time how her body had become fuller, more feminine, how her breasts were slightly swollen and the curve of her hips more rounded.

Not that she'd put on any weight, she assured herself. It was just different. She smiled and bit her lip, thinking of the baby growing inside her still-flat belly. A rush of new emotion flowed through her.

Then with another tiny sigh, determined not to linger on a future that could not be, she pinned up her long golden hair and climbed into the bath.

*　　*　　*

An hour later Victor was anxiously pacing the floor of the *grand salon* downstairs. Occasionally he glanced at the ornate ormolu clock, centred on the mantelpiece under the vast gilt mirror, while keeping his eyes trained on the stairs as well.

On the chime of eight Araminta began her descent of the majestic staircase. She had donned the beautiful gown which fitted her perfectly and flowed to the ground. In her hand she held the small evening purse. She wore little make up, just a touch of lipgloss and a sweep of mascara. Her hair was brushed and gleaming, shimmering like silken strands under the crystal chandelier.

And Victor held his breath as he watched her, so elegant and lovely, descending the stairs, controlling an impulse to rush forward and take her in his arms. This was the mother of his child, he reflected, the woman he loved but who needed to be wooed. So instead he waited for her to reach the bottom step before moving forward to greet her.

As she stepped into the marble hall Araminta saw Victor, perfectly attired in black tie, coming forward to greet her, and she swallowed. He looked so incredibly handsome, so smooth, dark and sophisticated.

No wonder he'd changed his mind about her.

'Good evening,' he said formally, raising her hand to his lips. 'Welcome again to the Château d'Ambrumenil.'

Araminta shuddered involuntarily as his skin grazed hers and the all too familiar memories surfaced.

'Good evening,' she responded, hoping she sounded sufficiently calm, cool and collected.

'Come in. Can I offer you a soft drink?' he asked, showing her into the *salon*—a beautiful if somewhat formally decorated room, decked with Aubusson carpets, brocade and gilt furnishings and a number of Old Masters on the walls—and moving towards a silver ice bucket where a bottle of Cristal stood chilling.

'That would be very nice, thank you,' she replied with barely a smile, searching the room for any other guests. Apparently she was the first to arrive.

Victor poured two drinks, then joined her near the fireplace. 'Please, sit down,' he said, handing her the soft drink and indicating one of the Louis XVI armchairs.

'Thank you,' Araminta murmured, and perched on the edge of the chair.

'I see the dress fits you to perfection,' he murmured, his eyes coursing over her, leaving her flushed despite her desire to stay completely unaffected by the sight of him, by the closeness wreaking havoc with her system.

'Yes. It was most kind of you to think of it. I had no idea you were planning a formal dinner party. How many guests are there?'

'Two.'

'Ah.'

Conversation did not seem to be getting very far, she reflected, taking a sip.

'Did you have a good flight?'

'Excellent, thank you.' This was awful, far worse than she'd anticipated. It was like talking to a perfect stranger.

'Dinner will be served in ten minutes.'

'Really? What about the other guests?' she asked.

'Araminta, I have already told you there are only two guests,' he murmured, his eyes turning darker, the lines of his face suddenly intense.

'Wh-what do you mean?' she said, suddenly nervous.

'That you and I are dining alone, my dear, *à deux*.'

'Oh, but surely—' She swallowed and took a quick gulp of her soft drink that nearly made her choke.

'I feel we have a lot to say to one another,' he continued, leaning against the mantelpiece, arm casually resting there.

'I don't. I think we said all we had to say the other night. In fact, I'm not quite sure why you asked me to come here,' she muttered, trying to stay calm although her heart was lurching and a thin film of perspiration beaded her upper lip.

'Aren't you?' His eyes bored into her now, belying his casual stance. He looked rather like a leopard, ready to pounce. 'I would have said rather that we hadn't even begun talking, *querida*.'

'Victor, if this is your idea of a joke I'm afraid I find it most unfunny,' Araminta said, in a voice that reminded her distinctly of how Lady Drusilla might have spoken.

'A joke? I hardly think so.' Posing the glass flute on the mantelpiece, he moved to her side and sat down in the chair next to her.

How she wished he'd keep his distance, that the scent of his musky aftershave wouldn't reach her quite so intensely, that she could keep that light-headed delicious tingle far removed from her body.

'Araminta, I think it's time you and I faced the truth,' he said, stretching out his arm and laying his hand on hers.

'I don't know what you mean,' she jabbered nervously. 'I made it very clear the other night that—'

'Let's forget the other night.'

'Oh, please, Victor,' she said, suddenly unable to stand this much longer. 'I can't bear it. Just leave me alone. Why did you ask me here?' she exclaimed, suddenly losing control as tears rose and she willed herself not to cry.

'Because of this,' he replied.

In a swift movement he was out of the chair and raising her into his arms. Before she could move he pulled her against him, snaked his hand into the mass of golden hair at her neck and drew her head back, his black shining eyes gazing down possessively into hers.

'Did you think for one moment that I would allow you to disappear from my life, *minha linda*? That I would contemplate leaving the woman I love to her own devices? Do you for one instant believe that I would allow another man to take you in his arms as I am taking you now?'

Araminta's pulse galloped. 'You love me?' she blurted out, surprise and doubt written in her eyes.

'Oh, my darling, my silly, ridiculous darling. Can't you tell, *querida*, how much I love you? I know it took me a while to understand, and a kick in the pants from Pearce to make me realise it, but of course I love you.'

'Well, that's hardly very complimentary,' she murmured, smiling, trying to stifle the rush of joy, surprise and relief overwhelming her.

'Complimentary or not, it's the truth, my love. That's why I brought you here.' He loosened his grip and slipped his arms around her waist, smiling down at her now, his eyes filled with a new intense expression she'd never seen before but which she recognised for what it was.

'Why exactly *did* you bring me here?' she whispered, unable to take her eyes from his face, unable to believe that this was really happening.

'Before I tell you, may I ask you a question?' he said in a gentler tone.

'All right,' she murmured, disappointed when he took a step backwards, leaving her standing in the middle of the Aubusson carpet wondering what he was going to do next.

'In that case, here goes. I'm not very good at this, I'm afraid. I've never done it before.' He smiled wryly at her, and before her unbelieving eyes fell on one knee. 'Will you, Araminta, my love, do me the honour of becoming my wife?' From his pocket Victor produced a sparkling diamond ring which he held up.

'I—' Araminta gasped, tears of joy and tenderness blinding her.

'All you need to say is yes,' Victor murmured, taking her left hand and slipping the ring onto her engagement finger. 'Well?' he asked, his eyes laughing now as he looked up at her. 'I don't know how long I can carry on in this pose, *querida*, without feeling completely idiotic.'

Araminta laughed and cried all at once. 'Yes,' she whispered, biting her lip and staring unbelieving at the man she loved holding her hand.

'Good. That's settled, then,' he said, rising relieved from the floor. 'May I kiss the future *comtesse*?'

Before she could answer, or absorb this information, Victor enveloped her in his arms and his lips came down on hers. He held her close and pressed his hands into the small of her back, making her feel the intensity of his desire while his tongue played havoc with hers.

Oh, it was glorious, wonderful, unique to be back in his arms, where she knew she belonged. And all at once Araminta threw her arms about his neck and kissed him back hard, needing to feel every inch of him. She thrust her fingers into his glorious black hair and gloried in it, caught between desire and laughter, joy and delight.

Then Victor swooped her into his arms, and in several masterful strides they were climbing the stairs.

'What about dinner?' she whispered, kissing his ear.

'Damn dinner. It'll just have to wait.'

Next thing she knew they were in a large bedroom and she was being laid in the middle of a vast silk canopied bed. Eyes glued to one another, they undressed quickly, each too anxious to feel the other to concede to any niceties as a pile of clothes littered the floor and Victor joined her between the deliciously cool sheets.

'*Meu amor,*' he whispered, suddenly slowing the pace and allowing his fingers to trace from her throat down her ribcage until they reached her belly. Then with new tenderness he lowered his head and kissed her there. 'Our child,' he muttered between feather kisses. 'Our baby. Oh, Araminta, I'm so happy, so proud of it, of us, of all that awaits us, now and in the future.'

'Victor,' she murmured, heart full, arching as his fingers trailed slowly lower, reaching down between her thighs, gently parting her, caressing, needing to feel her soft, warm, liquid response.

Then, as she gasped out his name, he entered her, long and slow, with a tenderness so great that Araminta thought she would weep from sheer joy and delight.

And together they journeyed on a newly discovered ocean of emotion, rising and falling on the swell, reaching out and discovering new heights of passion and sensation to which neither had been privileged before.

After, when it was finally over, when at last he lay with his head on her breast and she cradled him there, feeling his spent body moulding hers, Araminta knew what true happiness was.

And that nothing could equal it. Ever.

Victor took Araminta's arm and walked her to the dining room.

'So why,' she finally asked, her curiosity piqued, 'did you want to bring me here specifically?'

'For the very good reason that I wanted you to see your future home, *querida.*'

'My future home? You mean you want to come and live here?'

'Yes.' Stopping as they reached the hall, he looked into her eyes and murmured, 'I do.'

'But I don't understand. Why did you buy Le Moulin?'

'It's a long story,' he said with a sigh. 'Basically, I didn't want to share this place with Isabella. It has too many childhood memories, too many family connotations. I bought Le Moulin to keep her happy, and away from what I subconsciously must have been preserving for this moment.'

'You mean she never came here?'

'Never. The only other woman who used to come here was my mother—the late *comtesse*.'

'Comtesse?'

'Yes. My mother was a French countess. When I inherited this château and these lands from her I also inherited the title. Up until now I have never used it, but that is something I plan to change.'

'Why?'

'Because I want you to become my *comtesse*.'

'Oh, Victor.' She laughed, glancing down at the beautiful engagement ring which fitted her perfectly. 'I still haven't thanked you properly for this lovely ring.'

'It was my mother's engagement ring,' he murmured, caressing her cheek. 'It is appropriate that you should have it.'

Araminta smiled at him and raised her lips to his.

'I shall endeavour to do it justice.'

'Of that I have no doubt,' he said with an arrogant laugh, sweeping her into his arms and bestowing a long kiss on her lips. 'But now, my dear, it's getting late. And we must eat, or tomorrow we shall be without a cook.'

Rolling her eyes lovingly and taking his arm, Araminta fell into step beside him, knowing there was little use arguing. For, she admitted finally, glancing tenderly at his proud profile, she loved him and would love him always.

Just the way he was.

M.B.

4/05

ML